For

LITERARY YOURS

SOUTHERN SOIL

BOOK 1

L.A. BORUFF

COVEY PUBLISHING

Thank you for being a fan!

♡ — *L.A. Boruff*

LITERARY YOURS

COVEY PUBLISHING, LLC

Published by Covey Publishing, LLC

PO Box 550219, Gastonia, NC 28055-0219

Copyright © 2017 by L.A. Boruff

All rights reserved. No part of this publication may be reproduced, distributed, or transmitted in any form or by any means, including photocopying, recording, or other electronic or mechanical methods, without the prior written permission of the writer, except in the case of brief quotations embodied in critical reviews and certain other noncommercial uses permitted by copyright law.

This is a work of fiction. Names, characters, businesses, places, events and incidents are either the products of the author's imagination or used in a fictitious manner. Any resemblance to actual persons, living or dead, or actual events is purely coincidental.

Cover Design Copyright © 2017 Covey Publishing, LLC

Book Design by Covey Publishing, www.coveypublishing.com

Copy Editing by Covey Publishing, LLC

Printed in the United States of America.

ISBN: 978-1-948185-17-2

First Printing, 2018

ALSO BY L.A. BORUFF

Southern Soil

Literary Yours

CONTENTS

Chapter One	1
Chapter Two	20
Chapter Three	36
Chapter Four	56
Chapter Five	77
Chapter Six	99
Chapter Seven	116
Chapter Eight	130
Chapter Nine	145
Chapter Ten	158
Chapter Eleven	175
Chapter Twelve	196
Chapter Thirteen	215
Chapter Fourteen	236
Epilogue	215

ACKNOWLEDGEMENT

This is my second attempt at fiction, and I'm quite proud of it. But it wouldn't exist without the help of several people. First, Jennifer – thank you for your constant help and fantastic ideas. This book would literally not exist without you. Wayne – thank you for taking care of all the other aspects of our lives so I could spend hours writing and editing. Mom, Claire, Hennah, Megggggan – thank you for your advice and time spent helping me make the book SO much better.

DEDICATION

For Annie and Momo

CHAPTER ONE

The judge pushed her small, wire-rimmed glasses up her nose. She sat at the head of a conference room table for the informal, preliminary meeting, but she still made an imposing figure as she addressed my lawyer. "It appears, Mr. Saniger, your client's father left her before preparing her to run Asche Publishing." She peered down her nose at me, over the top of her frames.

"She deserves a chance to try, Your Honor." Charles, my lawyer, turned and nodded, encouraging me to make my statement. My stomach roiled at Charles's urging, but I stood up, spine straight and head held high. I kept my voice even as I responded. She needed to believe me an adult, not a petulant child. My stepmother painted her statements, given moments before, in such a way I almost questioned my own ability. I took a deep breath to steady myself and gave my prepared speech.

"This company has been in my family for three generations. My parents raised me to take over." A single tear rolled down my cheek as I gripped the side of the table.

"Unfortunately, my father died before I could complete my degree. I have two years left. I'm asking to be afforded time to finish school as I run my company." My voice strengthened as I continued. "My stepmother doesn't have the best interests of the company or the Asche legacy in mind. I'm content to work with the board to appoint an interim CEO, but I should be a deciding vote. The interim CEO isn't a man my father or I would've chosen." My voice broke. "I have dreams for this company, and there is plenty of support already there to help me achieve those dreams." I let out the last of the air in my lungs, thankful to be finished.

"Mrs. Asche, do you have anything to add?" The judge eyed my stepmother, sitting adjacent to me, with disapproval. I hoped it was disapproval.

"As a matter of fact, I do. I *am* an Asche now. I'm a part of the legacy. I worked alongside William for seven years before he died. I want the company to gr—"

"You didn't! He created a fake job for you so you'd get out of his hair," I cried out. Her superior tone and blatant lies got to me. Six months had passed since my father died, six months since I'd seen her, but the sight of my stepmother's face and the sound of her voice made the pain fresh. Charles grabbed my arm and shushed me as the judge directed her gaze to me, unquestionably with disapproval. She didn't say a word. I shrank under her glare.

The judge remained silent for a few moments as she rifled through some papers. "Mr. Saniger, I need to review all of the documents the plaintiff provided. There are several testimonies from your board about why she's more fit to run the company. And you need time to speak to your client's professors and further prepare your arguments." She paused and pursed her lips. "I'm going to adjourn this meeting until after the first of the year. I want to see both parties present their statements then." She stopped and addressed the lawyers on both sides. "Please prepare your briefs and send them to my clerk. Keep in mind, we'll be closed all of next week for Thanksgiving."

My chest expanded as I drew in one more deep breath and released it slowly. I could handle it. I had until the new year to get my act—and my case—together. As I gathered my purse and other belongings, the judge's reedy voice rang in my ears. "Miss Asche, if I could have a word with you."

I glanced around the conference room in surprise. Charles and I were the only ones left. My stepmother and her team had hightailed it out of there. A moment of fear caused my voice to warble. "Yes, Your Honor?"

She paused a moment and cocked her head at me. "I wanted to talk to both you and your lawyer for a moment." Her kindly smile relieved a bit of the churning in my gut. A little, not all. "In the interest of this case and to make sure the trial runs as fairly as possible, I wondered if you'd given any consideration to your counsel situation."

Her question threw me. "My counsel situation?" I asked, giving Charles a side-long glance.

"Yes." She smiled at Charles fondly. "Charles and I go way back. We've been friends for many years, and until now, we've been fortunate enough to make arrangements to avoid overlapping cases. But with his unexpected return to the courtroom, this one slipped through."

Charles smiled. "It was a surprise to see you on the other side today, Jean. A nice surprise." I grinned at Charles. Was he flirting?

The judge, Jean, eyeballed me. "Yes, ah, that's the reason for my conversation. I'm going to have to recuse myself if this matter goes to trial. I can stand in for the preliminary hearings and basic decisions. But when it comes to a court case, I'm too closely associated with your lawyer."

My jaw dropped as I floundered over how to respond. Charles, bless his heart, took over. He succeeded in further astonishing me with his words.

"It *was* a surprise to see you, but as soon as I did, I knew this would occur. I've already made a mental list of trusted firms who might be willing to take on her case. I'll get on that tonight." I sighed in relief. Charles would take care of me, even if he couldn't be my lawyer.

Jean gave Charles a bright smile. "You always were quick to adjust, Charles. Very well then." She turned to me, her face impassive once again. "I'll expect clear and convincing evidence from both sides. Prepare your representation." With a friendly nod and goodbye to Charles, she left the conference room.

"Charles," I asked my friend and mentor, "why would you not let her recuse? Why pull yourself out instead?" I didn't want to lose my case over something silly.

"You beautiful child. I've been retired too long to take on such an important case. But I've kept up with who's who in the city. We'll get you the best." He reached over and squeezed my shoulder with a gnarled hand.

Before we headed to the parking garage, I took a moment and hugged him close, grateful for his humility. As we walked down the hall toward our vehicle, someone behind me let out an irritated huff.

It was a sound I had been intimately familiar with during my childhood. Most often brought out anytime I entered a room without my father present; it would then be followed by a litany of my transgressions, usually pertaining to my appearance.

I pivoted to find my stepmother and her abhorrent son and daughter staring a hole through me. *You're an adult. You don't have to subject yourself to her vitriol!* I gently tugged on Charles's arm. "Let's go. We've much to discuss."

"Of course, Ellie. You can drop me off at home, and I'll give you those names," Charles replied sweetly, acknowledging my hope of taking the high road. We turned toward my car with every intention of ignoring my stepmother, but she wouldn't let us go.

"You'll never get this company from me, little girl." Her nasal voice grated on my nerves, and I flinched as bile rose in my throat. I'd hoped to never cross her path again.

"Not one word to her, Ellie." Charles put his arm around me and pushed past the biggest mistake my father ever made. "Raquel, I urge you to stop speaking to my client. Anything you have to say can go through your lawyer," Charles spoke over his shoulder.

"You old fool. You'll never win!" Raquel's voice sent me straight to my thirteen-year-old self's emotions—anger, betrayal, and eventually, defeat. Raquel made my life miserable for five years. Her interruption reminded me of the day my father delivered the worst news since my mother died.

"Ellie!" My father called up the stairs. "Can you come down here a minute?" I tossed my blanket aside and uncurled from my spot in my window seat, setting my mom's copy of Little Women down before trotting downstairs.

I stopped short at the entrance to his study. His girlfriend sat in the room, perched stiffly in his wingback chair. "Yes, Dad?" I asked, voice as polite as I could muster. "Hello, Raquel." She nodded at me with a waspish smile.

I wasn't thrilled he had a girlfriend, especially that particular girlfriend. She acted as sweet as syrup to me when he was around, but as soon as he wasn't, she changed. She hadn't said or done anything rude, more an overall feeling she projected toward me.

My dad gave me a blistering smile. "Ellie-Bellie, I have great news!"

"Dad," I whispered urgently. "I asked you not to call me that." When mom died, I wanted him to stop calling me names she also called me. He never gave up, though. I didn't usually mind, but I

hated it in front of her.

"Sorry, sorry. Raquel and I have news!" He grabbed her hand and flipped it over. I stared at the huge rock on her left ring finger, and my world crashed down around me as he said the words. "We are getting married!"

My first instinct, screaming and storming out of the room, would get me grounded. I couldn't bring myself to smile though. I settled for a grin. "Congratulations." I tried to adjust my features to grin without grimacing.

The excited expression on Dad's face faded. "It's a surprise, and we haven't dated long. But Raquel has two children around your age, and I think you need more feminine influences in your life." He released her hand and walked to the doorway to take mine. "You can be friends with her daughter, Michelle. And, I care deeply for Raquel. I ask that you give our new family a chance." His eyes pleaded with me; He wanted it to work and wanted me to get on board.

I glanced at Raquel and dropped my voice to a whisper. "But, Dad. What about mom?" I spoke as softly as I could.

Pain slashed through my father's eyes, and I regretted mentioning her. He coughed once. "Ellie, Mom's been gone for five years. You need someone to teach you the ins and outs of being a woman. I can't do that." He pulled me in for a bear hug. "I wish I could."

"Of course, Daddy. I'll give it a chance. Congratulations." Tears prickled my eyes as I pulled out of my father's arms. I needed to escape before Raquel saw me cry. The whole time I'd been in the room she hadn't said one word to me.

"Excuse me; I have to go get…" I trailed off and hoped they

didn't question me. I whirled and ran out of the room.

How could he consider remarrying? Only five years had passed since I stood between my father and my best friend, and watched my mother's body being lowered into the ground.

A few minutes after I threw myself onto my bed to sob, I heard a knock at my door. "Come in, Daddy," I called, wiping the tears off of my face.

Raquel pushed my bedroom door open and stepped inside. She shut the door with her heel as she glanced around the room. Her upper lip curled at the small pile of clothes in the corner of the room beside my bathroom door.

"Cynthia," she said severely. "We should talk." I jerked off the bed and hastily neatened my hair.

"I don't go by Cynthia. I go by Ellie." She'd called me Cynthia since my dad told her my full name. I couldn't imagine why she came to my room.

"Yes, well. I wanted to make sure we're on the same page." I didn't say a word at first, but my expression said every thought running through my mind—mainly her craziness. What page did she mean?

"I don't know what you mean, Raquel." I'd never been rude or mean to her, but she appeared to be angry with me. "Did I do something to upset you?" Something about her demeanor, her stiff, cold posture, made me a little afraid of her answer.

"You made it perfectly clear that you have no intention of respecting the marriage between your father and me." She sniffed delicately, eyeballing my messy bed. She walked in her high heels over to my bookcase and glanced at the titles.

"I didn't mean to do that. It was a surprise. I'm sure we'll all

get along fine." I didn't believe for a red-hot second we'd get along, but I knew I must be respectful. My mother would've been upset if I spoke impolitely to my elders. I fought tears as I considered what my mother would think about Raquel.

She ran a finger over one of the shelves then studied the dust on her finger. I hadn't done a deep cleaning in several weeks, and I never let the cleaning lady in my room. It was my space, and I'd keep it clean—except during summer break I'd been a bit lazy.

"I won't allow lies in my home." She turned to me and brushed the dust off of her finger. "You'll follow my rules, or you'll regret it. As long as you do, you'll have no problems." She made her way to the door. I stood in front of my bed, wide-eyed and terrified of the impeccably dressed woman. "Am I clear?"

"Yes ma'am," I said. I didn't know what else I could say. My dad obviously thought she was awesome. I'd already told him she gave me the creeps, and he rolled his eyes and told me not to be melodramatic.

She walked out of the room and shut the door behind her. The closing of the door had finality to it, like she closed off my life as I knew it. I grabbed the phone by my bed and dialed my best friend. He'd help me figure out how to deal with this new development.

I was so shocked in the beginning of their marriage that I didn't say anything to my father—a decision I'd later come to regret.

Charles's hand warmed my arm as he led me away from Raquel. His presence comforted me a bit. We soon reached the car, and I continued to seethe as I lowered myself into the driver's seat. After a few moments of attempting and failing to collect myself, Charles reached over and loosened my bruising grip from the steering wheel.

"She's a horrible woman!" I flapped my hands in an attempt to dissipate my anger. "What did he ever see in her?" The years I'd been out of the house hadn't tampered my repressed emotions as well as I hoped. Waves of anger cascaded over my body, causing my stomach to be upset. My neck burned, and the flames crept up my cheeks.

Charles snorted. "She was different with him. She's a charming, alluring woman when she has her sights set on marrying a rich, lonely widower." He let out a long sigh and motioned me to put the car in drive. "They seemed to be in love, but any woman devoted to your father would've loved you. As far as I'm concerned, that's how true love works, and I have a fair bit of experience in that area. You'll experience it one day, Ellie." He sighed and gazed out the window, lost in his memories. "Your mother and father had it. A more perfect couple I've rarely seen. If it's possible, they might've been even more compatible than my dear, late wife and me."

When upset, Charles rambled. I smiled at him and let him run his steam until we hit the road.

"That woman would run your company into the ground. But we're not going to let her. I've got several options for names that I'd let run my own trial. I'll call some of them tonight and have them get in touch with you to set up a meeting."

I pulled up to Charles's apartment building. As the concierge approached, I leaned in for a hug. "I love you,

Charles. Thank you for everything. Let me know when you get the meeting. I'll clear my schedule to go whenever they want to meet."

"Love you, too, girly. I'm so proud of you, and I know your father would be."

I waved to him as he walked into his building and headed home. The ten-minute drive to my own downtown building wasn't enough time to let my stomach ease. It knotted up again when I pulled up to my building and spotted a society reporter lurking near the front entrance. "Ha," I muttered. "You won't get any pictures of me today." I pulled my car into the underground garage, far from prying eyes.

My father's death and the succession of his company was a hot story in the society pages, as my stepbeast and her hell spawn were frequently featured. I, thankfully, wasn't—usually.

I opened the side door to find the doorman waiting on me. "It's getting worse, miss." Roger worried excessively and watched constantly for reporters.

"Yes, it is. And I'm afraid this is only the beginning." I peered out the tinted windows at the cameraman. "I hope when the case settles they stop sniffing around me. I don't do anything exciting enough for them to want to write about me."

"Miss? I can't imagine they wouldn't want to know about you. The beautiful, orphaned daughter of the richest man in the city?"

Uncomfortable with compliments, his comment made

me laugh nervously. My stepmother made it clear I was the ugly step sister, not the belle of the ball. "Oh, poo." I waved him off. "I'm frumpy and boring. But anyway, how is that new grandbaby of yours?"

His face lit up with pride only a grandparent could possess. "He's a stinker, Miss Asche! Growing like a weed. He'll be passing to the end zone in no time." Typical of Texas to be planning a child's gridiron career from birth.

Grinning a goodbye to the endearing man, I took the elevator. I brushed a little lint off of my pin-striped skirt and admired the shape of my ankles in the high heels picked out to match the ensemble.

I dug around in my purse until I found a clip for my blond hair and pinned it up. I appreciated the air on my still-heated neck. I couldn't wait to grab my latest romance novel and try to forget the ridiculous day. I'd deal with choosing new lawyers tomorrow.

The elevator reached the fifth floor, and I scurried to my unit. My building, converted into luxury apartments from an old warehouse, was a trendy place to live; though, I didn't care a bit about its trendiness factor.

Mine was one of two apartments on my floor. A suave, confident, classically handsome bachelor lived in the other. I'd embarrassed myself around him every time I encountered him, usually by saying something stupid. Something about him and his two best friends put me off-kilter. My dad would say I was twitterpated.

His short brown hair and chiseled features captured my eye and left me speechless. A little taller than me, his muscles proved he hit the gym on a regular basis. Even though I avoided him, my eyes drifted to his apartment door, hoping to catch a glimpse.

Think of the devil and damn if he doesn't appear. The soft snick of a knob turning snapped my focus to his door as he stepped out of his apartment before I reached for my keys to enter my own. "Ma'am. Doing all right today?" His deep voice purred, like a well-tuned muscle car. I trembled at the sound and regretted not having my keys ready when I exited the elevator.

"Hello. I'm fine, thank you for asking." I avoided eye contact and fumbled for my keys. I finally slipped inside before I stumbled through any further conversation. I wasn't shy, but he threw me straight out of my element. It didn't help he tried to talk to me every time we passed in the hall.

I slipped one heel off and jumped when a knock rang through my silent apartment. I whirled around. "Ma'am, it's me," my neighbor's voice was muffled by the thick door. I pressed my hands against my abdomen as butterflies attacked my stomach. Slipping my heel back on, I took a deep breath and promised myself I wouldn't act like a total dork.

I flung open the door forcefully. "Yes, hi, uh... can I help you?" My voice was high and nervous. I couldn't remember his name. I couldn't remember *my* name as I ogled his broad chest covered in a flannel shirt. My throat dried out when I caught sight of his snug jeans. His five o'clock shadow and short cropped hair topped off his cowboy ensemble. The only thing he needed was a Stetson and some cowboy boots.

He chuckled. "I'm Arch," he reminded me. "I didn't mean to startle you. You're Ellie, right?"

"No, you didn't startle me. I have a lot on my mind." *Don't blurt out your woes; he doesn't want to hear that.* "And yes, I'm Ellie."

"I wanted to invite you over. I'm having a small party tonight. Nothing major, a few cocktails and some music. We'd love to see you there." My mouth gaped. He wanted me to come to a party at his house. What a perfect end to the day. Embarrass myself in front of all his friends. I'd find a way to do it.

"I'll try. I, uh, made plans with my friend, Todd, tonight," I lied.

"Bring him along. He's the rather... uh, colorful guy you hang around with?" He put one hand on my doorframe and leaned.

I couldn't help but laugh. "Yeah, that's Todd. Colorful is an understatement. He's my best friend, has been for years." I couldn't think fast enough to come up with another excuse not to go to the party. If truth be told, part of me did want to go. "Do you mind if I bring his husband, Rick, as well?"

"Of course not! See you between seven and eight." He flashed me a charming smile and sauntered down the hall toward the elevators.

A grin spread across my face as I stood in my doorway and watched him walk away. Even though I'd likely embarrass myself in front of everyone, it was still bound to be fun. I ran inside to get ready.

My phone chirped in my purse as I kicked off my pinching heels. To the closet with those feet-eaters. I grabbed my phone and glanced at the screen. Charles moved quickly.

Charles: Ellie, I spoke to one of the senior partners at Beaumont, Morales, and Lawson. They're willing to take your case.

Ellie: That's wonderful! Were they your first choice?

Charles: Yes. They're one of the best firms in town.

He explained they were finishing up paperwork from their last successful case, and they'd meet with me in one week, the day before Thanksgiving. I thanked him for the fast work, wrote down the details for the office, and then called Todd about the party.

The call went to voicemail, so I tried texting.

Ellie: Todd, I need you! My oh-my-god neighbor...

Todd: WHAT DID HE DO?

The phone started ringing before I could reply. "Took you long enough," I said with relief.

"*Wear This, Not That* is on a marathon. I can't be bothered when I'm watching my show."

I rolled my eyes. "I know, I know, but you know what a big day this was for me."

"I was never worried, the bitch has no case. Your dad left you the company. End of story."

I sighed. "It's not that simple."

"Why the hell not?" His voice was indignant.

"She implied the judge has statements from members of the board saying she's more fit to run the company and still keep it in the family." I grimaced but made my response non-committal. "Hopefully, they decide she can't be considered a real Asche."

"Did you tell the judge she's a fake whore who wanted your dad for his money?"

I laughed at his bold attitude. "The opportunity didn't present itself."

"Did you do your hair today?" I could picture him pursing his lips.

"I left it down." He didn't respond for a full five seconds. "Hello? Earth to Todd."

"I'll be right over. You're hopeless. I know you've already ripped off half of what you wore. Don't take off any more, I want to see you."

I sighed and hung the phone up. I knew better than to argue. I plopped down onto my couch and waited. Within five minutes, a key rattled in the doorknob. I didn't bother changing positions. I'd known Todd since elementary school; he'd seen me in far more embarrassing situations, including the first time I tried alcohol and every breakup since Chad Tuttle said I had girl germs in the second grade.

Todd entered the room in a flourish of gardenia perfume and a silk house robe. "Nice of you to dress for me," I said.

"Oh, please. You interrupted my show, and I came up anyway. I love you, and you damn well know it. Rick and I were snuggling." Todd lived two floors down with his husband. They'd only dated about a month before getting married, but that was two years ago. Their love was sweet and a little gag-worthy, even if they did get some flack from their parents for getting married freshman year of college. I adored them together.

I sat up a little. "I know. Now, give it to me so I can tell you about the unbelievable afternoon I've had."

He eyed me critically. "You wore a seven hundred dollar suit and three hundred dollar shoes." He eyeballed my heels lying on the floor beside my suit jacket. "You wore all these nice things I painstakingly picked out for you, but you didn't even wear makeup or blow out your hair?" His voice rose in pitch with his irritation.

"Todd! That isn't me! I'm a bookworm! I'm a pudgy, bespectacled nerd! I don't wear makeup." He plopped down beside me with a sigh.

"You're beautiful. What do I have to do to convince you? Raquel spent so much time and attention on how gorgeous her kids were, it made you feel invisible." He pulled me into his side. "You're not invisible, and there's nothing wrong with gussying up every once in a while."

"I know. I do. I'm not invisible. I'm smart and fully capable of running the publishing company I grew up in. The board will teach me whatever I don't already know." I wanted to change the subject and needed him to understand.

"Of course they'll teach you. So tell me what all happened today, and don't think I've forgotten about the mysterious something your neighbor did." He began brushing his fingers through my hair.

"Raquel got to the board, that's what happened." Todd stiffened. "Not all of them." I reassured him. "But, enough of them that the judge wants me to prove I can handle the company. She could take this company from me." I fought the tears gathering in my eyes. I didn't want to let my father down by allowing our legacy to go to the most horrible woman I knew.

"Well, we won't let that happen." He squeezed me.

"I have to get a new lawyer." I stuck my lip out. "Charles said it would be best. He says he's been out of the game a little too long."

"Is he handling the choosing of the new lawyer?"

"Yeah. He's already lined someone up." I threw my head back, suddenly exhausted.

"Too bad." He turned his head, nose in the air. He was hiding something and wanted me to ask him about it.

"What's too bad?" I gave him what he wanted.

"I happened to run into that hunky neighbor of yours a few days ago and pried a little. Turns out he's a lawyer—a successful one if my quick Internet search is to be believed."

I gasped. "You're joking!"

"Nope. Now, what juicy dish do you have about him?" He leaned back to stare me down until I talked. I took a moment to contemplate the new information. Maybe I shouldn't go to the party. If he was a good lawyer, I might want him to help me, and that could be a conflict of interest.

My mouth curled up. I knew he'd be excited about this news. "I gave in." He blinked at me. "So, Arch has been inviting me to parties for months, you know?" He nodded his head vigorously. "You, Rick, and I have an invitation for a small party at Arch's apartment tonight at seven-ish." He blinked a few more times as his mouth dropped open. "And I said yes."

He jumped up, clapping his hands. "We have three hours!"

I put my hands up. "No, Todd. I'm dressing in jeans and a t-shirt. This thing is low key."

Todd deflated. "Makeup?"

"No," I said.

He eyeballed my head. "Let me play with your hair."

I sighed. "I'll let you do that, but only because it feels so good to have you brushing and twisting and whatever else you do."

"Okay. I'm going home. You take a nap; recover a little from your day." He stood and headed for my front door. "I'll be back in two hours to play with your hair and talk you into wearing mascara." I rolled my eyes at him as he made his exit. He was a mess, but I loved him dearly.

CHAPTER TWO

True to his word, Todd came back, Rick in tow, with enough time to brush my hair until it shined. He sprayed something on it and twisted it into a complicated braid. Having it off my neck would keep me from fiddling with it all night.

I straightened my hot pink tee and turned to my friends. "You ready?" My hands fluttered a little at my sides, betraying my nervousness.

"Sweetie, we can't go!" Todd exclaimed.

"What?" Panic laced my voice. I'd already told Arch we would be there, and I didn't know if I could do it without my security blanket, Todd.

"I thought I told you earlier. Rick got us movie tickets for tonight. We may pop in after the movie, but we have to run now or we'll be late." Todd looked like someone ran over his favorite puppy. "I did want to go with you, but we've had this date made for weeks."

"Who throws a party on a Wednesday night?" Rick asked.

I threw my hands up. "I don't know, I never would. But I've already said I'd be there, so I guess I have to go." I didn't want to be rude to my neighbor. I'd make a quick appearance and then go home. My reward would be the eye candy sure to be present at the shindig.

My friends made their exit, giving me quick kisses and apologies. I stared at Arch's apartment door with foreboding before slamming my door shut and leaning my head against it. I'd wait and go a little later, as if I tore myself away from something important. *Damn my nerves.*

I parked myself on the couch and stared at the clock on my wall. I let time tick down with only my cell phone to distract me. Playing a solitaire game helped. Finally, the clock said eight thirty, and I stood.

At eight forty, I finally opened my door and stepped out into the hall. The idea popped into my head that Arch could have a surveillance system like mine, a monitor mounted beside my door giving a view of the hallway, which spurred me to knock on his door without dawdling. I would've hated for him to catch me hovering in the hallway on his security monitor.

A man I'd passed in the hall but never spoken to opened the door. His platinum blond, honey-streaked hair was natural, not dyed. He had sun-kissed, surfer-dude good looks, with gunmetal blue eyes. His most noticeable feature was his size. Six or seven inches taller than me, he had broad shoulders and massive arms. He filled out the doorway so I couldn't see inside the apartment.

"Hi." I began with a squeak. "I'm Ellie. Arch invited me." My hands, firmly tucked into my back pockets, itched to twist something nervously.

Belatedly, I noticed music spilling out of the apartment and laughter and talking inside. My stomach clenched at the idea of pasting on a fake smile for all of those people. In the back of my mind, I pictured Arch's warm invitation and that bolstered my nerve. I did want to get to know him a little better, given we were neighbors.

Tall, blond, and Norse-god-lookalike cracked a smile that'd knock out a gaggle of old church ladies. "You're the neighbor! Come on in, Arch hoped you'd show."

I chuckled a little. *Maybe he thinks I'm mysterious.* I suppressed a snort. *Yeah, right.*

His apartment was nothing like I'd imagined. I'd always pictured modern decor with lots of black and white coloring and uncomfortable furniture. "Who decorated this place?" I asked, amazed.

"Uh," Blondie studied the apartment like he'd never noticed the decor. "Arch did, I think."

"It's awesome. I love it." I gazed around at what could only be described as autumn comfort. His walls were cream with burnt orange accents. He had dark brown furniture, and it was all overstuffed and appeared comfortable. His entertainment center and other wood furniture lightened up the room a bit with a blond color. "What sort of wood is this?" I asked, indicating the coffee table and other pieces.

He gave me a blank stare. Arch saved any further awkward conversation by walking up. "She likes your decorating style, man," said Blondie, before clapping Arch on the shoulder and walking over to a small group of people sitting at the dining table.

My smile was a little crooked. "I'm here," I said with mock enthusiasm.

"I'm glad you came, Ellie. I've been dying to find out more about you, but you're always in a hurry."

My hands fluttered to my throat. "I'm so sorry. I can be a little shy, but I didn't mean to be rude." I cursed my bashful behavior. He held my gaze with his piercing hazel eyes.

"You weren't rude. You're cute." I blushed red, startled by the compliment. He blurted it out there like it was no big deal. It was a big deal to me.

"Thanks. So, do you always throw random Wednesday night parties?" I smiled to show I didn't mean it as a criticism.

"Not usually, no. Normally, we have to be in the office bright and early through the week and a lot of weekends, too. We've been working round the clock the past few years." He puffed his chest a little, proud. "We're celebrating a big accomplishment at work. We won a big case."

"What do you do?" Todd told me Arch's profession but I didn't want him to know I'd gossiped about him.

"I'm a senior partner at Beaumont, Morales, and

Lawson." He motioned me over to a table filled with cocktail fixings. "Are you old enough to drink? I didn't even think about that."

My stomach clenched in confusion as I replayed the names he mentioned. I was sure I had the names wrong. I pulled out my phone to double check while I answered his question. "Uh, yeah, I just had my twenty-first birthday." I pulled up my text from Charles. Sure enough, it was the same law firm. "Arch, this is crazy, but I think your firm took on my case today."

His eyebrows lifted in surprise. "I'd forgotten you were in the middle of a suit. We read about you in the paper the other day. You're fighting for your dad's company, aren't you?"

I ignored the pang in my gut at the mention of my father. "Yeah. It's a mess." I hoped they'd read the article about my volunteering, even though it painted me in a ludicrous light, and not the articles from the society pages about *The Publishing Princess*. That's what the press was calling me. *Ridiculous.*

"Our civil partners would be handling a case like that. We won't have anything to do with it besides the intake." He offered me a glass of white wine, which I accepted gratefully. I needed a little bit of fake courage. "How long ago did your father pass?" His voice was sympathetic.

"Only six months. It's still raw. I'd rather not talk about it tonight." I gave him a wavering smile. If I put on a brave face, it often made me braver inside. Or, it at least made it easier to tuck the immense pain into a corner.

He squeezed my arm. "You bet. So, since we're the names on the building, one of us does the intake on every case our firm takes. I'm sure I'll find an appointment with you on my calendar when I go back to work." His wide grin made my breath catch in my throat.

"A week from today, but I don't know who with." I sipped the sweet wine and glanced around the room at the other guests. Besides the two friends I'd noticed at Arch's apartment in the past, only a handful of men and women played cards at the dining room table.

"I'll make sure it's me so you're comfortable." He smiled down at me. "Our law firm covers a wide spectrum of litigation. We have six different lawyers currently practicing with us, each of whom excels in their own specializations." He poured several liquids into a container and began to shake vigorously. "We heard about your case and wanted to approach you, but we'd never step on Charles Saniger's toes. He's respected in this town."

Charles was more well-known than I'd realized. "Should I be here?" I would've hated to lose my second lawyer because of a technicality.

"Yeah it's fine. We're criminal lawyers. None of our civil partners are here. As long as we don't have anything to do with your actual case, there's no conflict of interest." Arch wandered over to the couch and sat down.

Since I didn't know anyone else in the room, I followed him. "Want to play a little Mario Kart?" he asked.

Here was my chance to embarrass myself. "Sure, but I have to warn you: I'm terrible at any and every video game

I've ever tried."

Arch let out a boyish laugh. "I'll take it easy on you." He handed me a black controller, and I tried to remember which buttons did what. The last time I played the game, Todd and I were teenagers.

Half an hour and ten races later, I'd maintained my spot in last place, and two other guys joined us. Wes was the massive blond I met at the door. The other, Gray, was a slender—yet also muscular—Latino man with hair longer than mine. It reached halfway down his back and was glossy like a hair product commercial. His voice had the smooth lilt of someone used to switching flawlessly between Spanish and English.

Every time the game was paused, I stopped myself from staring out of the corner of my eye at the three guys sitting around me. It was surreal to be playing a video game with three hot guys

They teased me like I was one of the group, which helped relax me considerably. I even started teasing them back.

"Ouch. I thought you were supposed to be good at this game," I teased Gray when his character fell into a ravine.

"Laugh it up. I've already lapped you once." His accent was Southern, the same as his two friends.

I spent a second too long watching him, and when I turned to the game, I was driving into a wall. Correcting myself, I focused on the race for the last lap and managed to end the game in second-to-last place, instead of last.

"Hey! I didn't come in last. It's a small victory." I pumped my fist into the air.

My wine glass set on the coffee table, forgotten. I grabbed it and slurped the rest of the wine, suddenly thirsty.

"Can I get you some more?" Wes offered. He reached his hand out for my glass.

"Thanks. Yes, but only one more. I have no desire to wake up with a hangover." I smiled up at him as he rose. For such a big person, I expected him to be a bit clumsy, but he moved with grace.

Gray was putting our controllers in the entertainment cabinet when a song came on I hadn't heard in years. I squealed. "I love this song." It was a ballad from a boy band popular when I was a freshman in high school. I leaned back on the couch, head back, and hummed along. "This takes me back."

When I opened my eyes, Arch stared at me like I'd grown a baboon butt on my forehead. Gray stood in front of the entertainment center with an equally bewildered expression on his face. "What?" I asked.

"I'm not sure what *their* problem is, but I've never heard this song in my life. How old are you?" Wes spoke from behind me as he walked around the couch to hand me the wine.

The song was iconic. Everyone my age, plus or minus three or so years, would recognize it. "I'm twenty-one. How old are *you*?" I said a little prayer they weren't two decades older than me with youthful faces.

Arch answered for them. "We're all twenty-eight. Gray is the youngest, and Wes the oldest."

I gawked at them. "You say that like you're brothers. Usually, only siblings talk like that." The only way they were siblings was if their dad was naughty and got all their moms pregnant at the same time. Their appearances and features were completely different.

They laughed, like I told a big joke. "We're not biological brothers, but we grew up together. We might as well be blood."

That made a little more sense. If they'd known each other all their lives, they probably thought like brothers. "If you don't know this song, I can't help you. You've missed out."

A debate started about the best kind of music to listen to. Turns out all three were fans of metal music. "If you all like metal, then why are we listening to pop now?"

Arch discreetly pointed to one of the women sitting at the table playing cards. "It's her iPod. She took over when she got here and plugged it in." He shrugged. "It's one night of music we don't care for. We can deal." He glanced at his friends. "Besides, we would've been arguing over what *kind* of metal to listen to."

I was impressed with his laid back attitude. I sipped my wine and contemplated the guys I'd dated. Most were adamant about music choices. "I know most people roll their eyes when someone says this, but I'm pretty eclectic. I love pop music, but I also love metal, rock, and a little bit of country. And, I've been known to listen to a little classical or Broadway hits."

My gaze was on Gray when I finished talking, and his face was frozen like he was trying hard not to roll his eyes. "Name one metal band you like." His voice was skeptical, and his attitude was a little uppity for me, like how so-called metal heads acted.

"Black Sabbath is my favorite and always will be." I fought the urge to raise one eyebrow and purse my lips. I schooled my features into a neutral, calm expression. "Before you ask, my favorite song is War Pigs, followed by Fairies Wear Boots."

Gray's skeptical expression broke, and he chuckled. I said a small prayer of thanks to the music gods. I'd dated a guy the year before that worshipped Black Sabbath. I did like them, but I would've never known a single song name without his obsession. I made a mental note to send him a Christmas card.

"Nice," Wes said. "I'm impressed." He sat beside me on the couch again and grinned appreciatively. "So, you're eclectic, but do you love music?"

"The only thing I love more than music is reading. I wish I could play an instrument." I sang all through high school, but never had an inclination to try to learn to play.

"It's never too late to learn," said Arch. "Gray could teach you to play guitar."

Gray shook his head. "Heck no, man. I tried to teach a girl one time, and I do *not* have the patience."

I laughed at his honesty. "I don't have the time now. I like to spend time volunteering, plus school and school work takes up a lot of my time." I rolled my eyes. "And now the lawsuit. Maybe one day I will, but for now, I'll listen and be a music fan." I sipped my wine, determined to make it last. No rough morning for me.

"Where do you go to school?" Arch seemed genuinely interested in my life.

"I'm a junior at Southern." I fought a smile, flattered and proud of my school. I'd earned the grades for an ivy league but never did enough extracurricular to be of interest to them. I volunteered some in high school, but not as much as I'd been doing lately. Southern was a great alternative to an ivy.

Gray's face lit up. "You're kidding!" He leaned forward. "I do guest lectures for their pre-law students!"

I laughed, but then got serious. "So now I'm at a party with partners from the law firm I'm about to hire and a professor at my college?" Disappointment clenched my chest. "I guess I'd better go home."

Gray threw up his hands. "No, wait. You're civil, right? Not criminal?" I gave him a curt nod and a sad smile. "Then we're golden. I'm a guest at the college. Not on the payroll or anything. Please, stay."

"If someone needed to leave over the college thing, I'd make Gray go," Arch deadpanned. His face was so serious that I smiled at Gray sympathetically.

Gray punched Arch in the arm. "Whatever, man." Arch's serious expression broke, and they both busted out laughing.

Before we could get back into our conversation, Arch

got called over to the card players. "Whoops. I guess I've been ignoring them," he whispered to me before he got up. "I'll return in a few." I grinned at his back, thankful for his hospitality. I was comfortable enough with his friends by then. I'd even stopped gawking at them.

Gray, Wes, and I shared a short awkward silence after Arch made his exit. I scrambled to find something to talk about. "Ahh, Gray?"

"Yeah?" He questioned.

"What's it short for?" Surely it was a nickname.

"Nothing. My parents liked the name."

I tried to pull my foot out of my mouth. "I like it." I raised my glass to my lips to avoid saying anything more. Gray laughed at my expression. I tried for a whoops face. Hopefully, I pulled it off.

Wes interjected, "Wesley."

I smiled at him. "I like your name, too, Wes."

He buffed his nails on his shirt. "Of course you do." The tension broke with his antics. "Ellie, would you like something to eat?"

Wes was a natural host. He kept trying to make sure I didn't need anything. "No, I'm good, thanks." I got up to stretch my legs and glanced around the room. Arch sat at the table, but only two people remained. I checked my phone and found we'd chatted about music and random bits of nothing for two hours. It was after ten.

Arch put the cards they played in their case. The two women at the table got up and waved to the three of us standing by the couches. As they walked out the door, I noticed they were holding hands. Definitely not a love interest of Arch's then, not that I cared about his love interests.

I swallowed the last bit of my wine and walked the glass to the kitchen sink. Arch's floor plan was even more open than mine. A half-wall separated my kitchen from my living area, but only an island divided his.

I turned to find Arch, Wes, and Gray sitting at the kitchen table. "I should head out, too." I didn't want to leave, but I also didn't want to be the only person left at a party. The three of them didn't count, as they were joined at the hip. I leaned against the kitchen island.

"Oh, come on," protested Arch. "I was about to suggest a movie." He pointed toward the shelves of movies on his entertainment unit. "Pick one out."

I stared at the shelves of movies with longing. I hadn't expected to have so much fun. But Todd's voice whispered in my ear, "Always leave them wanting more."

Sighing, I shook my head. "Sorry guys. I promised I'd go by the shelter and walk the cat early tomorrow."

Gray opened his mouth, but then he snapped it shut. He gave me a concerned glance before speaking. "Don't you mean walk the dog?" His tone said, 'Are you okay? You're talking crazy.'

Laughter bubbled out of my mouth. "I'm considering adopting this cat. He's a Maine Coon, and someone leash trained him like a dog. If he's not walked two or three times a day he gets cranky." I did love that cat.

Wes's face lit up. "I have a cat. He's a huge, orange

tabby named Lemmy." He grinned the way only pet owners could—like their pet was their baby—and also a little like a maniac. "You should definitely adopt the shelter kitty. What's his name?"

"I, uh…" I paused for dramatic effect. "I've been calling him Satan. He's a little bit evil." I downplayed it because he was a lot evil.

I shouldn't have worried; they all laughed. Apparently, naming a cat after the devil was acceptable in their social circles.

"I'd love to meet Satan," said Wes. Arch and Gray chimed in the same.

"If I do decide to adopt him, you'll be the first people I call." I smiled indulgently at them. They weren't just pretty faces, they were truly nice guys. *I've never seen a girl here with Arch, but surely the other two have girlfriends.* I rolled my eyes. What did I care if they had girlfriends or not?

"I'll walk you home," Wes said. He stood and held out his arm like a cotillion escort. I said my goodbyes to Gray and thanked Arch for inviting me. Then, I took Wes's arm like it was a normal occurrence for me to be escorted five feet from Arch's door to mine.

While I dug my key out of my pocket, I tried to convince myself Wes was being big-brotherly and not romantic. Because if he was being romantic… I could get used to that sort of chivalry.

I opened my door. "Thank you for walking me home. I've never felt safer in my own hallway." I gave him a goofy grin to show I was joking. He didn't know me enough yet to read the tone of my voice.

"Actually, Ellie, I wanted to ask you something." He rubbed his neck, blond hair barely reaching his hand.

"Sure, what's up?" Maybe he wanted to go volunteer with me. I'd managed to bring in lots of volunteers over the years.

"Can I ask you out to dinner sometime?" He smiled at me with his panty-melting smile again. He must've known the effect it had on women because he flashed it at the perfect time to elicit a 'yes' from me.

"I'm about to start a case with your firm. Wouldn't that be a conflict of interest?" As much as I'd like to get to know him, I couldn't afford to do anything to damage my case.

"No, actually. We wouldn't be able to discuss your case, and I wouldn't be able to have anything to do with it at work, but as long as we followed the rules, it would be legal and ethical." His face turned hopeful. "So, dinner?"

I'd been asked out plenty of times in my life, but only by guys more on my playing field. Physically, I was out of my element with Wes and his friends. *Who are you kidding? He's gorgeous, and given his job, intelligent. And, he loves cats. That's enough to start with. Say yes.* "Sure, Wes, we can get dinner sometime." I lowered my eyes, a little embarrassed at how fast I agreed to a date with a man I'd just met.

"Great." He sounded excited. "How about tomorrow night?"

Holy crow! That gave me no time to prepare. "Yeah, that's fine. Could I see your phone?" He handed over his cell, and I programmed it with my number. "Text me in the morning, and we'll decide where," I said as I returned the phone.

I slipped into my apartment and turned on my monitor. Wes did the typical guy 'yes' motion, pumping his hand and pulling up one knee as he made his way across the hall, like a teenager whose crush told him she'd go to prom with him.

Once I locked the door and set the alarm, I made my way to my bedroom. Grabbing my phone, I texted Todd to see if the movie was over. I couldn't wait to tell him about my date. Before I could type, a text came through from a number I didn't know.

Unknown: This is Wes. I wanted you to have my number. Sleep well.

I stared at the words for several seconds before typing in a reply.

Ellie: Have fun with your brothers. Talk to you tomorrow.

I forgot my text to Todd. I threw myself on my bed and stared at the ceiling with a huge smile on my face. I crumbled when I realized my dad hadn't crossed my mind more than once or twice all evening. For the first time in six months, he didn't dominate my thoughts.

Guilt set in as I hugged a pillow with my dad's shirt on it. It still smelled like his aftershave and cigars. I dreaded the day the scent faded. I finally found my way to sleep on a pillow damp with tears.

CHAPTER THREE

My alarm made a horrible buzzing sound, making me want to throw it out of my fifth-floor window. I cracked one eye open and glared across the room at the alarm clock. I learned years ago to keep it out of arm's reach, or I'd never get out of bed in the morning. I let out a little scream. "I'm up! God, shut up." I only drank two glasses of wine the night before, but my head pounded like I downed the entire bottle.

I rolled out of bed and shuffled over to my dresser to shut the alarm up. Next stop, coffee pot. Thanks to an automatic timer, the smell of it brewing woke me up enough to prevent me from climbing back in bed. I continued my morning zombie shuffle through the living room and into my kitchen to the fresh pot on my counter. *Sweet nectar.* I poured a cup and added a generous helping of pumpkin coffee creamer.

I curled up in the plush chair beside my living room window and yawned as I watched the city wake up. As much as I hated mornings, I needed a few minutes to let my brain catch up to the day. I always allowed myself an extra thirty minutes to get moving.

Coffee crept into my veins and loaned me a semblance of humanity when my phone went off in my bedroom. The catchy Madonna song told me it was Todd calling.

I didn't bother with a greeting. "Please tell me you have time to come up and talk to me while I get ready. I've got to go walk Satan."

"I'm already in the elevator. Bye!" He hung up, and I grinned. I should've known he'd be dying to get the scoop on Arch's party.

Swigging the last of my coffee, I skipped to my bathroom, in a suddenly excellent mood. Todd had his own key and would let himself in. I turned on the taps for a shower and twirled around as I put toothpaste on my toothbrush. I stripped and hopped into the shower, brushing as I went.

The bathroom door burst open. It would've scared the pants off of me, except I was already naked. My best friend sighed dramatically. "You're going to make me sit in here and talk to you while you take a six-hundred degree shower, aren't you?" I couldn't see him, but I knew he rolled his eyes to the ceiling like I'd asked him to give up his firstborn child.

"No, you can wait in my bedroom. I won't be long, I shaved yesterday." I peeked my head out from behind the shower curtain. "But I have so much to tell you." I sighed and decided to tease him. "I have a date." I shut the curtain again. "Go wait in my bedroom."

"Dear sweet baby Buddha, I know you don't expect me to wait out there now." The sound of the toilet lid crashing down made me laugh. "I want the entire story. Now."

As I showered, I walked him through the details of the party. By the time I got out, I'd only made it through our video game playing.

A half wall separated the shower area from the rest of my bathroom. It was my favorite part of the room. I was able to get out, dry off, and still maintain a modicum of modesty.

I didn't know why I bothered, though. Todd had seen me naked many times before. We'd been attached at the hip for sixteen years. I was no longer embarrassed by nudity when it came to him.

I continued my story over the wall as I dried. Donning my favorite worn out robe, I made my way to the other half of the bathroom as I told him about Gray being a guest lecturer.

To his credit, he didn't interrupt once, even though I knew he burned to know which guy asked me out. I continued my story as I walked into my closet to dress. I didn't come to the juicy part until I took my hair out of its towel and brushed out the tangles.

"So then, I made my exit," I said evasively. Todd's face turned red, and I avoided laughing at him.

He took my hairbrush from me. "Woman! Great story, tell it again." He continued after an exaggerated eye roll. "But nowhere, not one freaking time, did you mention a date!" He twirled me around and began artfully detangling my long hair without any pain. He was a hair and makeup genius. When he finished his business degree and opened his spa, he'd be in high demand.

I stretched my neck and leaned my head back to allow him to brush from the front to the back and finally told him the rest of the story. "...and he's supposed to text me today to set up the restaurant for the date tonight."

Todd stopped brushing. "So you're going on a date tonight with a gorgeous and interesting man, you've got Satan this morning, and how many classes today?"

"Just the one." I took the brush and put my customary part in my hair. It would dry on my way to the shelter. "It's at ten, then I'm done for the day."

"Thank goodness. Text me as you're parking here this afternoon, and I'll meet you back up here." He whirled out of the bedroom and I followed, ready to head out. "My only class today is at eight, so I'll be home before you. We can play in your closet for a while." He put on huge puppy-dog eyes and stuck out his bottom lip. "How much are you going to let me do this time?"

I scrutinized his pout. I wanted to dress nice for the date, but I still wanted to look like me. "Um, you can put my hair up again, nothing too fancy, and put on some mascara and lip gloss. Low key." I glanced toward my closet. "And my dress depends on what restaurant he suggests."

We made our way into my living room and I checked my phone. It was after seven; I needed to hurry. The shelter was a thirty-minute drive, and I liked to spend at least two hours there. Throwing a second cup of coffee into a travel mug, I locked the apartment and headed to the garage. Todd, on his way to his morning class, accompanied me.

"How's Rick?" I asked. He was probably already at his office.

"Good," Todd sighed. "He's starting that end of year mess, you know. I'll be on my own for several weeks."

Rick, an accountant, spent several weeks at the end of every year making sure all the details were taken care of. It meant late nights and a dejected Todd. I did my best to distract him from missing his man.

We hugged at the car, and I set off to play with my favorite Satan-cat. My day dragged by; my evening plans weighed heavily on my mind. It was the first time I'd even considered dating since my dad died, and my lack of a guilty conscience surprised me. The highlight of my morning was deciding to adopt Satan. I zoned out in class, thinking about the sweet—meaning evil—kitty. I decided all at once I had to have him.

My class finally ended, and I raced to the shelter to pick up my new roommate. I surpassed the normal shelter waiting period due to my frequent visits there. They all knew I adored Satan and were thrilled with the match.

I approached his cage on my tippy toes. He always

knew I was coming and waited at the door to his small home. I'd never before succeeded in sneaking up on him, but he wasn't used to me coming in the middle of the day. I always came in the morning. I turned the corner as quietly as I possibly could and burst out laughing because my giant, black and white bundle of fluff waited for me at the cage door.

"Can you smell me coming, big guy? You always know!" I'd asked the other shelter workers, and they said he never budged from his napping position when they walked past his cage. I grabbed his leash and reached inside the cage to clip it him on it. As soon as I opened his door, he jumped gracefully down to the ground and started down the hall.

Satan led me to the front doors. Once in the lobby, he sat patiently while I said my goodbyes to the workers. I opened the front door, and he walked straight to my car. "It must be my smell, you clever boy. How else would you know which car is mine?"

I'd already stopped off at a pet store on the way to get Satan, so my back seat was filled with the things I needed for my new friend, including a carrying cage. I picked him up and tried to put him in the cage, but he yowled angrily.

His face turned toward mine, and though he donned an expression of pure evil, suddenly he seemed to be pleading. "You don't want to go in a cage, do you?" I asked as if he could understand me.

It was against my better judgment to leave him loose. If he got under my feet, I could wreck. But I placed him in the front passenger seat, and he curled up into a ball. I stared at him until he lifted his head and stared back. "You better stay there, Satan. Don't you dare move." Conceding to my demand, he laid his head down.

This damn cat can't possibly understand me. I closed his door and walked around to the driver side. He glanced at me when I got in and then put his head on his paws. I made a crazy face at him, then focused on the road.

I kept glancing down at Satan on the drive home, but he never moved. I would've sworn he slept, except every time I spoke to him, he twitched his ears.

I texted Todd once I parked, then loaded my arms up with the plethora of kitty paraphernalia. "I went a little overboard," I said to the fuzz ball as he hopped delicately from the car. I grabbed Satan's leash, and for once, he followed me instead of leading the way.

He sniffed the elevator apprehensively. I stood inside, holding the door open with one foot, gently tugging his leash. "C'mon, dude. It won't hurt you, I promise." He gave me a reproachful glare and meowed pitifully. In the end, I had to give his leash a stronger tug before he would creep in.

He hunkered down with the movement of the car and bolted out when the doors opened on the fifth floor.

Todd was about to put his key in my door as the elevator opened. He turned toward me then dropped his jaw in surprise. "What the hell is that? Is that Satan?" He burst out laughing as the massive cat pulled me toward him.

Satan ran straight for Todd, who dropped into a crouch. Instead of offering to help me with my bags and the cage, Todd, with *my* new cat wrapping himself around his legs, was lost in baby talk. "I'm going to pull on his leash and knock you both over. Get the door, you big softie."

Todd grabbed Satan and hefted him up to his shoulder before reaching around me to open the door. I dumped everything on my couch. Todd shut the door and let Satan off of his leash. Satan began exploring my apartment, starting with my bedroom. I took his litter box and set it up in the laundry room beside the kitchen.

"So, dating a new guy wasn't enough for you for one day? You decided to finally bring Satan home?" Todd rifled through the bags of toys, treats, and medicines.

"Yeah, I don't know." I plopped down beside him. "It occurred to me—what was I waiting on? Why couldn't I have a cat? I'm home enough. They don't need the twenty-four-seven maintenance a dog needs."

Todd opened the toys and put them in the little paw-covered bin I bought. He meticulously placed all the trash in an empty bag. He couldn't help but be neat.

I pulled out my phone and handed it to Todd so he could read the text I received in class. As soon as I walked out the classroom door I'd replied to it.

Wes: How do you feel about going to Blossoms for dinner?

Ellie: I love that restaurant. Their pasta dishes are delicious.

Wes: We're on then. Six okay?

Ellie: Perfect. Meet me at my apartment, I have a surprise.

Todd turned to me questioningly. "What surprise?"

I arched one eyebrow at him. "The. Cat. What else? I told you he has a cat and got excited at the idea of me adopting Satan."

"Cynthia Eleanor Asche, did you adopt this cat to impress a guy?" Todd stood and put his hands on his hips. Since I was parentless, he took it upon himself to be my guiding light in life. Sometimes it was endearing. And sometimes, like then, it was infuriating.

"No, I didn't, Theodore Wilfred Anderson-Pate. I adopted Satan because if I could handle making a date, I could handle bringing home a new friend. It felt right." I stuck my nose in the air and resolved to ignore him.

I was distracted by Satan stalking out of my bedroom. He sat in the doorway and yowled. Todd and I both jerked our heads toward the loud cat. "What's your problem?" I asked the distraught feline.

At the same time, Todd said, "Poor, confused, sweet, widdle baby boy. Is hims confused? Uncle Toddy will show you where to find your potty times."

My anger with Todd flew straight out the window. I couldn't stay mad at a man who loved my new cat enough to speak to him so ridiculously. "Good grief, Todd," I said around my laughter. "I'll put his food to the kitchen. Show him that next."

I busied myself with Satan's food. Once Satan settled

in, Todd and I headed for my closet. Blossom's wasn't a fancy restaurant, so I could wear casual clothes. However, since Wes would be coming straight from the office, he'd be wearing a suit. Given the Texas fall evening would be chilly at worst, we settled on dark brown linen pants. I didn't need anything heavy. The top was a thin, baby blue sweater so I wouldn't have to fool with a jacket. For shoes, I opted for a low-heeled slip-on.

We wasted a little time playing with Satan, then an hour before Wes was due, I allowed Todd to twist my hair up with a silver clip and apply mascara. Three coats, to be exact. "Luckily, my little palette, your skin is perfection. You don't *need* makeup, never have. But, it would be fun to put it on such a flawless complexion," he said as he applied the sheer lip gloss, all I'd let him put on my lips.

At five thirty, he kissed my cheek and wished me luck. I sat on the edge of a kitchen chair in my pressed clothes, since I didn't want to wrinkle them. Todd found Satan and kissed him sixteen times—I counted—and told him he loved him before finally leaving.

"He already likes you more than me," I told the fuzzy boy, who sat on my couch licking his paws.

Fifteen minutes earlier than I expected, my doorbell rang. I flicked on my security monitor to find Wes waiting. Opening the door with a flourish, I gave him an instant view of my new friend on the couch. Satan stopped licking his paw and jumped to the floor as Wes entered the room.

He turned to me as I closed the door behind him. "You adopted him!" His smile was even more heart-stopping than the one he unleashed on me the night before.

"I realized I needed him in my life. So, I went after class and got him." Wes picked Satan up like it was no big deal he wore a two thousand dollar suit. I had to assume its cost—Todd would've known for sure.

Luckily for his expensive suit, I'd bought lint rollers at the pet store. He didn't seem to care a bit as he nuzzled Satan's soft neck. "This cat is so chill, Ellie. You picked a good one." Satan began to head butt him, and purring sounds reached me across the room. "My Lemmy will only allow cuddles when he wants cuddles. And not a moment longer." Wes grinned at me. "But, he's mine, and I love him."

I shook my head at the duo. "Okay, so now that I know you're a crazy old cat lady at heart... you hungry?" I walked over to Wes and smooched Satan's head. "Let's go eat."

Wes put the cat on the couch, and I handed him the lint roller. Long black and white fur clung to his suit jacket. "You'll get used to de-furring yourself every time you leave the house. Lemmy's fur is bright orange, and it shows up on everything," he explained as he rolled the sticky sheet over himself.

"I had a cat once before," I said, trying not to get sucked into another miserable memory of my stepmother. "She was a year old when she died. But, that's a sad story, and this is a happy day. I have a new cat, a new team of lawyers to win my case, and a new date." I slung my purse over my shoulder. "C'mon. I'm starving."

We made our way to the garage. "I'm guessing Arch gave you a key code for the garage doors?" I asked.

Wes laughed. "Yeah, he got tired of running downstairs constantly to let us in. So he talked to the building manager and got us our own codes. We're here more often than at our own houses half the time." He led the way to his car, a big, red, Chevy truck. "Arch is the closest to work, and we worked so many long days, we've crashed at his place quite often." He held the passenger door open for me.

"Thank you," I exclaimed. "Chivalry isn't dead, it seems." I teased him a little. Even in the South, most men didn't bother with opening doors.

By the time he'd appeared at my apartment door, my nerves had lessened, plus we had Satan to distract us. But as he walked around the truck to the driver's side, I pressed my hand to my stomach to calm the reawakened butterflies.

After climbing in, he turned on the powerful truck engine. I observed the clean interior and new-car smell. "New truck?" I asked.

"Yeah, I got it last month. We're finally at a point where we can pay ourselves. Arch bought an apartment full of new furniture, and I got a new truck. My apartment isn't nearly as nice as this one, but I'm more of a saver." He pointed to a black SUV. "That's Arch's new rig. Gray made a big purchase, too, but his is more practical." He trailed off as he pulled out of the garage.

"What do you drive?" he asked.

"An Accord. I love it. I've had it since I turned sixteen. It's time to upgrade, especially as much as I'm in the public eye, but I can't give her up. My dad gave her to me on my sixteenth birthday." I stared out the window, lost in the memory.

My birthday fell on a weekday that year. It was still hot in Texas at the beginning of October. Once Todd drove us home from school, we spent the afternoon beside his parent's pool. Dad was at work all day, so I certainly didn't want to spend the day in a house with my stepfamily.

"When's your stepmonster going to go to the spa?" Todd asked. She liked to spend weeks at a time at some fancy spa in Switzerland. It cost my dad a fortune, but he smiled indulgently at her every time she went.

I dreamed of the days she'd go. When she left, Michelle, her daughter, would go stay with her grandmother. Since my stepbrother, Mitch, left for college the year before, the house would be back to normal with me and dad living there.

Unfortunately, she hadn't mentioned the spa in a while.

"I don't know. Hopefully soon, so I can spend a week or two not having to hide in my room. Every time I leave the room, she finds some reason to criticize me or something to blame on me." I put my sunglasses up on my head and pouted at Todd. "It's getting worse. Tell me again how it'll be soon."

Todd pushed my sunglasses back onto my nose, and I rested my head against the lounge chair. "Ellie, doll, we're going to have an incredible time. You get your trust fund two years from today. I get mine two months before you do. If we can, we'll get you out of there before you're even eighteen. We'll get an apartment near campus, and I'll decorate it perfectly."

I began to imagine what an apartment decorated by Todd would look like. It wasn't pretty. "We'll make so many friends and have parties every weekend. And we'll have access to our money, so nobody can tell us what to wear, what to eat, where to go, or when to be where. The monster can't blame you for anything anymore." It sounded heavenly.

"We'll eat healthy foods and work out every day," he continued, "and meet gorgeous guys getting high-level degrees to challenge our excessive intellects. Then, we'll push them to the curb because we won't have time for their nonsense."

I laughed at his story. "Todd, you wouldn't hurt anyone's feelings. You're too nice."

"You don't know. I might. We'll be grown and svelte. We might also be mean. Hush." He handed me the sun block. "Time to reapply. One thing we won't have is skin cancer." I slathered the lotion on my skin as he continued.

"You'll get your dual major, English Lit and Business. And I'll get my MBA." I turned my head to watch him. He always talked with his hands. I watched him flail them around as he spoke. "Then, fresh off of a successful college career, you'll take over the company and fire the bitch, and I'll start my spa. And she won't be allowed in the door, no matter how much she tries to bribe my staff."

He paused when my cell phone rang—my dad. I checked the time, but it was only four. He should've been at work for another two hours. I answered quickly. "What's up, Dad, everything okay?"

"Where are you, Ellie?" he asked with an edge to his voice.

"Todd's." I kept it short. There was no telling what sort of story

my stepmother had concocted to get me in trouble. Best to wait and see.

"I need you to come home, please. You can bring Todd, but I need to talk to you." He disconnected as soon as he was done talking.

I turned to Todd and stood. "Dad wants me home and said you should come so we can talk." My heart sank. "He didn't even mention my birthday." I shuffled my feet, dreading what was coming as we walked three houses down. Raquel would have some horrible story, and Dad would believe every line of it. He thought I was a rebellious brat. He always talked about how disappointed in me he was.

Every time I tried to tell him how horribly she treated me, he chalked it up to more rebellious behavior on my part. She'd done a number on him. He never would've believed I could be so bad before he met her.

I trudged up the front stairs and opened the door. "Dad?" The large home made my voice echo. Immediately after moving in, Raquel took down the classy decor my mom left and replaced it with ostentatious junk. Her taste was horrible. It was minimalist meets safari jungle tour. Todd faked vomiting every time he looked at the zebra skin hanging on the wall.

"In here, Ellie," Dad called from the kitchen. Todd and I entered the kitchen to the sound of the garage door opening off the kitchen. Dad had a huge grin on his face, and my step mother looked like she'd sucked on a lemon for her lunch.

"What's going on?" I asked. I looked from Dad to Raquel with apprehension. What had him grinning?

"Can you go out to the garage please?" Dad asked politely.

Todd snickered behind me. "Dad, c'mon. What did I do this

time? Am I to have trashed the garage or something?" I dreaded the shoe dropping.

I felt a push from Todd behind me. "Just go out," he hissed. I sighed and made my way to the side door that led to the garage.

I poked my head out the door, expecting to see Raquel's Mercedes and Dad's Lexus. Instead, a white Honda Accord with dark tinted windows sat alone in the garage. A huge red bow was pasted to the hood. I looked into the kitchen to my dad. His face lit up with excitement, as if he had received a car himself. "Dad! I thought you forgot!" Tears sprang to my eyes.

"How could I forget your birthday, Ellie-Bellie? You're sixteen! Now, hop in, and I'll take you to the DMV to get your license."

The tears broke free and rolled down my cheeks. "Oh, Dad. I took driver's ed last semester. All I had to do was take the certificate by the DMV this morning, and I got my license. Todd took me before school."

Instead of being thankful for the car, my tears were because my own dad didn't know that I'd taken driver's ed. He hadn't taught me to drive. He'd checked out when he married Raquel.

I still remembered the father who taught me to read while hiding under his big, fancy desk in his office. I remembered the dad who taught me to swim and ride a bike. He painfully and embarrassingly taught me about having a period and where babies came from. I remembered the man that had an active role in my life. He was a shell of the man he used to be. I tried to imagine he was still the old dad, but sometimes he made it impossible to pretend.

"Take her out for a test drive then. Take Todd. You two have fun." He fiddled with his glasses, unsure what to say. I guessed he was realizing he should've known about my driver's education class. I

walked over and hugged him. Raquel rolled her eyes at me behind his back. Her venom spewed from her eyes. I'd pay for the car later.

Wes broke through my memories. "Earth to Ellie. Where'd you go?"

I laughed nervously. "I'm sorry, Wes. Since my dad died, I keep getting thrown into memories I'd long ago repressed. They say it's normal, but it's still unnerving." I realized we were almost at the restaurant. How long was I silent, reflecting my own past? "I'm so sorry I was rude."

"Hey, don't sweat it. You looked sad, so I didn't interrupt you for a while. I know grief when I see it." He took one hand off the steering wheel to give my knee a reassuring squeeze. "Maybe, one day, you'll feel like sharing memories with me. If tonight goes well, that is." His voice took on a teasing tone.

I shook off the ghost of the memory and tried to come up with something to talk about. "So… Tell me something about yourself, Wes."

He pulled into the restaurant lot and parked. "I work out."

"Man of few words. Okay. But, I already knew that." His physique left no question he spent a lot of time in the gym.

He laughed. "No, you don't understand. I love the gym. Lifting weights is a form of meditation for me. It relaxes me and chases stresses away." He shrugged. "Always has, since I was about thirteen."

"Okay, see, that's better." I smiled at him. "I know something significant about you now." I took off my seatbelt and opened my door before he could jump out and come around to do it for me.

He grunted at me as he met me at the front of the truck. "I thought you liked a chivalrous man?"

"Chivalry is hot, but I can let myself out of the car. Proving a point is all." I winked at him to ease the sting of my sass.

Dinner passed in a blur of excellent conversation and good food. I learned more about Wes, including he had five brothers and sisters, he was mainly Scandinavian and British, and a pet peeve was when people bounce their legs idly.

I'd let a few things about myself go, tit for tat, and told him a small bit about my stepmother. I glossed over the worst parts, of course. If ever I was completely honest, people got a tragic expression on their faces and went all sympathetic. I didn't want that from someone I wanted to date. He also asked me why I volunteered so often.

"I read that article about your volunteering," Wes said.

My eyes rolled themselves before I could stop them. "That article was too much."

"It sure did make you sound like a saint. Are you too good to be true?" he asked jokingly.

"God no. I'm a mess most days. I volunteer as a sort of tribute to my mother." I sipped the last of my dessert wine. I promised myself years ago I wouldn't skimp on eating while on a date, and I hadn't, not even for the insanely fit Wes.

"Your mother? She died, didn't she? It was mentioned

in the article." He wiped his mouth with his napkin. "How old were you?"

"I was eight. It was horrible and traumatic, but we knew it was coming. She had time to tell me what she wanted for me in life. One of the things she told me was I should always make time to volunteer for people and animals less fortunate than myself." I put my own napkin on the table, done with my meal. "So, I do. And I love it. It's incredibly rewarding to watch a child's eyes light up when the math finally clicks. Or an adult's excitement the first time they bring me a book and tell me they read it through by themselves." I grinned. "And, obviously, I love working with animals. It sounds terrible, but that's my favorite. They're so deserving."

"Your mom sounds like she was an awesome lady." Wes's eyes started to take on that poor-pitiful-Ellie quality, so I moved on.

"She was. But, again, this is a happy evening. Let's talk about something else."

We finished the evening with a walk around the botanical gardens. He took my hand, a nice gesture, toward the end of our walk. *Nice, hell. You got a zing the second he touched you. Don't be shy.* I ignored my inner bad girl, and we ended our date at my front door. Wes, a complete gentleman, didn't even kiss my cheek. He kissed my hand. "I had a lovely time, Ellie. I'll be texting you to plan something again. I promise you that."

I let out a little puff of air when his lips brushed my hand, and the zing came back ten times stronger with his words. He was a gentleman, hot, smart, and *damn* I wanted a second date.

I was tossing and turning in bed, unable to fall asleep, when my phone vibrated. I snatched it from my bedside table drawer.

Wes: I enjoyed our time together tonight.

Ellie: I did, too. Thank you for a wonderful date.

Wes: Goodnight, beautiful. I'll see you soon.

Ellie: Goodnight.

I drifted off, feeling beautiful and wanted, with a smile on my face.

CHAPTER FOUR

After two morning classes, Satan entertained me for most of Friday, when I wasn't hosting a meeting for adults considering obtaining their GEDs.

Wes sent two random texts while I was in class. One was a meme about cats, and the other was a picture of his cat, Lemmy. Every time my phone dinged, I snatched it up to check if it was him. Too often it was social media or emails coming through. Eventually, I changed his text tone so it would ring distinct when he sent a message.

Saturday morning dawned with no alarm clock for once. I took weekends off at the shelter. I couldn't figure out why I woke early. I had no reason to. A crash sounded in my kitchen. I bolted out of bed, wide awake and panicked. I kept one of my guns in my bedside table, and I slipped it out before pressing the panic button hidden in my headboard.

Keeping a low-key lifestyle didn't mean I should be unprepared. I was still a millionaire heiress to a large publishing company. I crept to my bedroom door and shut it as softly as I dared. Turning the lock with a soft click, I ran on tiptoe to my bathroom. There was no other way out, and I could shut and lock that door as well, giving the police time to show up. My panic button alerted the police and our building manager, so he'd be in the lobby, ready to give the officers a key.

I sat on the toilet with my revolver pointed toward the bathroom door. The only downside to the expensive wood was it was soundproof. I wouldn't know the intruder entered my bedroom unless he attempted to get into the bathroom. And, my panicked-self forgot my cell phone on the bedside table. I had no choice but to sit there and wait.

My leg bounced up and down. I tried to quell my nervousness, but the minutes ticked down slowly while I waited. I wasn't afraid of dying or being hurt. If anyone knocked on the bathroom door, I wouldn't hesitate to shoot them through it. The minutes of waiting were still terrifying.

I counted down four minutes and twenty-four seconds before someone knocked faintly on my bedroom door. I jumped up and pressed my ear against the bathroom door. "Police! Are you in there, Miss Asche?" I barely heard the shouts.

I'd allowed enough time for them to arrive at my apartment. The likelihood the police were out there was high, so I unlatched the bathroom lock. "I'm in here, and I have a gun! When you got my apartment key from my landlord, he was supposed to give you a safe word. Do you know it?" I called through the door.

The voice replied correctly, though muffled. "Desk Chair!" I unlocked the door, gun pointed at the floor. Officers streamed in around me and checked my room over, even though I'd been locked in. Arch came in behind them. "There's nobody here, Ellie. What happened?" I raised my eyebrows at him. I hadn't expected him to be there with the police.

I let out a sigh of relief and walked over to my dresser to put my gun up. "How bad is it out there? Is anything damaged?" I sat on the bed, exhausted.

A short, pudgy officer walked over to me to give his information. "Miss Asche, did you see an intruder?"

I shook my head. "No, a strange sound woke me. I didn't realize what it was until I heard a crash in the kitchen. I hit my panic button, grabbed my gun, and tiptoed over to lock my bedroom door. Then, I hid in the bathroom behind *that* locked door until you came."

Satan ran into my bedroom and jumped up on the bed beside me. I snatched him up. "I'm so glad you're safe, kitty-boy!"

"Ma'am," the officer said. "We saw no sign of forced entry. Your alarm was still engaged. There's no damage or mess in the house. The only sign of anything unusual is your kitchen garbage can has been knocked over, and the contents strewn across the floor." He fought a smile as I stared at him, floored. "Have you had your cat for long?"

I turned my head to peer down at Satan. He was curled up in my arms, purring, contentment on his evil face. "Satan! You didn't?" I scolded him. He twitched his tail at me.

"Ma'am?" I gazed at the officer. "Satan?" He stood there with laughter in his eyes, judging my poor kitty's name.

"Yes. He's the evilest kitty alive, would you look at him." I scratched his head, and he laid his ears back and purred louder. "You think my cat knocked over the trash can, and it freaked me out so I hit the panic button and caused this entire ruckus?"

The officer nodded his head, valiantly fighting laughter. The room cleared of any other officers, and Arch's face barely contained his mirth. I put Satan down to check out the apartment.

They were right. The only problem was the trash can in the kitchen. "You can both go ahead and laugh. You're right. It was Satan."

Not only did Arch and the officer crack up with belly-busting laughter, it came from the hall, too. I stuck my head out my front door. Four more officers stood out there, doubled over, laughing their stress away.

I turned to the officer inside. "At least I provided some comic relief for your officers today." My cheeks were fireballs. Embarrassed didn't begin to cover my emotions.

"Please don't feel bad." The officer finally contained his levity enough to speak to me again. "I've got three cats. You learn to recognize two sounds. One, the sound of the garbage can crashing to the floor. And two, the sound a cat makes before they throw up. It's distinctive."

I thanked him for coming out and apologized for my overreaction to my new cat's shenanigans. When he left, I turned to Arch with my hands covering my mouth. "I absolutely can't believe that happened," I mumbled through my fingers.

His laughter renewed. He gasped out around his guffaws, "That cat caused you to call the police! I can't wait to tell Wes, he'll love this." He collapsed onto my couch, still chuckling.

"How'd you even know they were here? Were they being loud?" How did he manage to show up at the perfect moment?

His eyes widened. He hadn't expected me to ask him that. "Yeah, okay." He sighed. "My power went out, and I was bored."

Nodding at him, I encouraged him to continue. What didn't he want to tell me?

"I… had my front door open, hoping to hear you get up and get your paper. I was going to bug you to let me come over and hang out here. My apartment was getting hot." He scratched his ankle idly and rolled his eyes. "I was hoping if you saw my door open, too, you'd come in to see why, and then invite me over so I wouldn't have to ask. There. Now, you know."

It was my turn to laugh at him. "That's nothing to be embarrassed about! If your power is out, come by and bum my TV or raid my fridge. Do you need to move anything from your fridge to mine?"

He laughed. "No, I talked to the power company, and they should be out within a couple of hours to turn it on. Turns out, I forgot to pay the bill." He smiled sheepishly at me. "Sometimes being an adult is hard, and I miss stuff."

I snorted. "We all do. Last month I almost forgot to pay my cell phone bill. It happens." I walked toward the kitchen. "You hungry?"

"Yes, please," he replied in a small voice as he followed me. He sat on one of the stools I kept on the living room side of the wall separating the living room from the kitchen. It was a great place to sit and talk to the cook without getting in their way.

I preheated the oven to make some frozen biscuits before walking out of the kitchen. "Be back," I said. I went to my bathroom to check I wasn't too scary after my morning fake-ordeal. Thankfully, my hair was only a little wild, and I didn't have any gross goop in my eyes. I was wearing respectable pajamas but changed into lounging clothes anyway. After brushing my teeth and hair, I made my way to the living room.

By the time I came out, Arch turned the TV on to the morning news. I sighed to myself. *He belongs on my couch.* I blinked my eyes and shook off the familiarity of him being comfortable in my home.

"How do you like your eggs, Arch?" I desperately needed a grocery store run, but I could make do with a few things on hand. At least I had plenty of eggs.

"I'm not picky. The only way I *don't* like them is runny." His eyes never left the news. A criminal lawyer would stay on top of the city's happenings, and the news outlets were one way to accomplish that.

I left him on his own and threw together a breakfast of eggs, biscuits, and fresh strawberries. When the biscuits came out of the oven, I called him over to my small kitchen table.

"Thank you so much, Ellie, this is awesome. I would've had cereal or a pop-tart at home." He shoveled eggs into his mouth with vigor. *I guess he likes them.*

"No problem. I'm an oatmeal and toast girl myself, but I figured I'd start your day off with something to stick to your ribs." I shook pepper over my eggs. I began eating as Arch took his last bites. His table manners needed some work.

He finished long before I did and took his plate to the kitchen. The sounds of the dishwasher being loaded tickled me. He needed table manners, but he got extra brownie points for cleaning the kitchen.

Once I finished, I added my plate to the dishwasher and joined Arch on the couch. He jumped up as soon as I sat down, and I looked at him in question. "I'm going to check on my power."

He came right back. "They've already turned it on. I don't want to overstay my welcome." He pointed to the notepad I kept on my desk in the corner. "I put my phone number there for you. If you ever need anything at all, text me." He turned to leave. "Shoot me a text now so I'll have your number, if you don't mind me having it."

I didn't mind. "I'll text you." I smiled at him. "Any time you need anything, let me know, neighbor." He gave me more warm fuzzies than a typical neighbor should. I sent the text off to him immediately.

He left, and I, of course, immediately called Todd to relay the hilarity of my morning. He enjoyed listening to Satan's antics and laughed along with me at Arch's embarrassment at his power outage dilemma.

"He should've knocked on the door when he realized his power was out. It might've woken you up before Satan did so you wouldn't have had to call the cops!" I laughed along with him because he was right.

I spent the rest of the day with Todd and Rick. We planned a nice dinner at their place, but I didn't want to leave Satan alone all evening. They came to my place instead. Unfortunately, my cupboards were bare. They brought all the food with them.

Sunday, I shopped. I stopped at the bulk warehouse store, the grocery store, the market, the pet store, and the drug store. By the time I made it home, it took four trips all the way upstairs to haul in my shopping.

After all the shopping, I rested. Reading time had been scarce the past several weeks. I curled up in my comfy window chair and lost myself in an epic fantasy novel. I jerked out of my fantasy world by the pinging of my phone.

Wes again. He sent me another picture of his Lemmy. After the picture, he asked when he could see me. I replied with a picture of Satan with a particularly evil expression and said, "I'll be in your office next week, then the holiday. Let's make plans later. I definitely want another date."

We texted back and forth for a few minutes about trivial things before promising we'd make plans the next week.

On Monday, I got a surprise text from Gray.

Unknown Number: Ellie?

Ellie: Maybe. Who's this?

Unknown Number: It's Gray.

Ellie: Well, hey! What's up? (and how'd you get my number?)

Gray: I snuck on Arch's phone while he was showering.

Ellie: So what's up?

Gray: I've had you on my mind since the party. Would you like to go listen to some music sometime?

Ellie: I'd love to! I'll see you this week; I have an appointment at your office, Wednesday.

Gray: Awesome. Talk to you soon. :)

Wednesday couldn't come fast enough. Excited to meet Wes again, I was also becoming intrigued by Gray. Arch, sneaky Arch, kept finding reasons to be in the hall or knock on my door—cup of sugar, cup of coffee. I knew he was making excuses to run into me when he knocked to ask if I knew the answer to his crossword puzzle clue.

"You could've texted me, Arch," I teased. I wasn't angry with him; it was kind of cute.

"I know, but then I wouldn't have gotten to pet

Satan." As soon as Arch sat down on the couch, Satan jumped into his lap.

"You only like me for my cat, don't you?" I laughed at Satan's contented purr. He certainly liked Arch and Wes. I couldn't wait to introduce him to Gray.

"You figured me out. I'm head over heels in love with your pretty kitty."

The innuendo struck me, and I tried not to die laughing. At first, I was embarrassed and didn't want him to know my mind could be that dirty. But when his eyes widened and he realized what he said, I couldn't help myself.

"Oh, my god, you walked into that!" I chortled as his face burned brightly.

Finally, Tuesday night arrived, and I lay in bed, too wired to go to sleep. I called Todd. "Hey, best friend."

"Hey, Ells. What's up?" he sounded bored.

"Wanna go with me to pay the retainer tomorrow and meet these guys for yourself?"

He sucked in a breath. "On one condition. You let me dress you first. *And* do your makeup." His voice turned triumphant, boredom gone.

I rolled my head back. "Urrrgh. Fine. You win. I'll let you make me pretty. The appointment is at eight."

"You're always pretty, darling. I'll make you gorgeous." He never failed to remind me I was beautiful.

It took me another hour after I said goodbye to Todd to fall asleep. I couldn't wait to encounter the intriguing men again.

I kicked at the tickling on my feet. Why were my feet tickly? I didn't want to open my eyes to see since I'd only closed them a few seconds before. There it was again, a tickle. I groaned my protest over being woken up. I didn't even care if it was a robber, as long as they let me sleep. Another tickle on my feet. "Stooooop it!!"

"Not today, sleeping beauty. Up and at 'em. You said I could do what I wanted to you this morning, and here I am."

"Todd Pate! What time is it? I need beauty sleep. And I didn't say you could do whatever you wanted. I said makeup."

"And hair."

"*Fine.*" I pulled the comforter over my head, which Todd, in turn, jerked completely off me. Satan ran growling out of the room. He didn't like being woken up either.

"Up!" Todd's voice grated that early in the morning.

I squinted one sleep-crusted eye at him. "What time is it?"

"Six. Here." Several cosmetic bottles fell onto the bed beside me. "Get in the shower."

He started out of my bedroom. "I'll make you breakfast. Oh! And shave your legs." After a wink over his shoulder, he sashayed out of the room. At least he dressed snazzy for the day, dapper in a dress shirt and slacks.

Thirty minutes later I was hairless in all the necessary places, polished, and moisturized. My bathroom saw me primp more in those thirty minutes than it had in the past six months, and we were only getting started. I trudged out of my bedroom wearing my old pink robe and slippers, hair in a towel.

Todd set a plate of eggs, bacon, and pineapple onto the table. While I stuffed my face, he removed my towel and squirted delicious smelling goo onto his hands and ran it through my thick hair. "Wha's 'at do?" I asked through my bacon.

"Volumizing. We're giving your hair more oomph." He pulled out a hair dryer and round brush and began pulling my hair up and out. "Please let me put highlights in your hair." Insisting I was his personal dress-up doll, he'd been trying to get his hands on my hair since my mom died. Before she died, we were too young to be allowed, and he'd been waiting on the day she gave permission. Once she was gone, I lost interest.

"No." I sipped my coffee. He'd made it perfectly, with hazelnut creamer.

"One day you'll change your mind, and when you realize what a few highlights can do, you'll be blown away. I promise."

"Whatever you say." I winked at him as he dried the sides of my hair.

I sat patiently, food gone, waiting for him to be satisfied with his work. When the moment came, he instructed me to stand in the middle of the room while he hair sprayed me into oblivion.

We made our way into my bathroom, to the plethora of makeup he'd purchased for me, most of which I'd never even opened. I was shocked at my reflection in the mirror. My hair appeared normal but better. Still long and straight, nothing special, except a little bigger, a little fuller, with a hint of a curl at the ends. It made a drastic difference without being obvious. I knew I'd never take the time to fix it every day though.

I sat on the toilet, face turned up, while Todd worked his magic. I tried to talk to him through clenched teeth so I wouldn't damage any of his work. "So, are you excited to see these guys?"

"I can't wait to get going. Why do you think I woke you up so damn early? You know I'm not a morning person!"

He'd been a notoriously late sleeper all his life. "I wondered what you were thinking."

"And then we're shopping."

"Tooodddddd!" I whined through a barely-open mouth.

"For me, not you! Rick's taking me to a fancy art show downtown this weekend. It's supposed to be romantic. I want to get some new clothes to surprise him."

"Okay. I won't complain, then." He used a brush to blend creamy foundation into my skin.

My mind strayed to my lawsuit as he blended. "Damn. I'll have to wear this mess every day if I head the company, won't I? It's the professional thing to do."

"I'm afraid so, dear."

"You'll have to teach me how to come up with a quick beauty routine. I'm not going full blown like this every single day." I didn't mind being professional and put together, but I was far too lazy to primp for hours a day.

"With your skin, you can get away with *much* less. It's like you don't even own pores." I furrowed my brow at the jealousy on his face.

"Okay. I can deal with that. And the hair?"

"Most days you can run some product through it, throw your head upside down, and blow dry." He fluffed my hair out

"Okay. I guess I'll do that. If it helps me with this company to have a more professional appearance, then I will, even though its complete bull I'm not being judged solely on my brain and work ethic." Women should be able to go to work without makeup and elaborate hairdos, like men did.

"Just wait. Fashion can be fun, you'll see." His voice raised in pitch with his excitement. He'd been trying to get me to act like a girl since my mom died.

He finished, and the final product looked like I didn't spend an hour getting ready but just rolled out of bed. My face was natural, but brighter and prettier. I hated how much I liked it.

"Ack. Let me throw some clothes on, and we can go." Todd let out a sharp laugh.

"Throw on some clothes? HA! Whatever. Go sit. I'll bring your clothes to you." I sat. A few minutes later, he exited the closet holding a pair of skinny jeans I'd never even tried on, and a red one shoulder draped shirt.

"You've got to give me *something* that's the normal me,

or they're going to know I'm trying too hard." I didn't want him to completely change me for one meeting.

"It never hurts to dress our best. And okay. I'll let you wear a looser cut of jeans."

"The straight leg, Todd. I mean it." He'd push me to wear what *he* wanted me to if I let him.

"Only if it's a new pair. You've worn the same three pair for ages." He crossed his arms and settled in to out-stubborn me.

My freshly plucked brow furrowed. "Agreed."

An hour and a half after Todd tickled me awake, I left in wedge heels that had never been on my feet, jeans and a shirt that had never been on my body, makeup that had never seen the light of day, and hair that had never bounced more happily. I hated to admit, but it was nice to know I looked my best, even if I hated the principle behind it.

We took Todd's little red sports car the five blocks to the high rise housing Beaumont, Morales, and Lawson. The underground parking garage led up into an atrium filled with plush couches and green plants. Todd noticed a gold plated tenant list and guided me over. The law firm was on the fourteenth floor.

My stomach clenched as we entered the crowded elevator. I grabbed Todd's hand, irritated at myself. Those three men were already under my skin. He gave me a reassuring squeeze. "Don't be nervous. I've got you," he whispered.

I took a deep breath. In through my nose and out

through my mouth. *Chill. They're your friends.* Nothing more and nothing less... Maybe something more. I needed to stop being nervous about the guys and focus on the severity of my errand to their office. It was time to win my case.

Todd stopped me outside the firm. He pulled a tube of clear gloss out of his pocket and dabbed a little on my lips. "You ready?"

"They're just lawyers." I rolled my eyes in mock irritation. "Let's get this over with. I'll meet the new people, write them a check, sign on the dotted line, and go."

Todd nodded the affirmative and opened the door. I swept into the room with my head held high. A platinum blond receptionist sat at an expensive oak desk. "Good morning!" she said, voice chirpy.

"Good morning," I replied formally. "I have an eight o'clock appointment with Arch."

"One moment, please." Blondie picked up her phone. "Mr. Beaumont, there's a woman here to see you. No sir, one moment." She turned her gaze to me. "Your name?"

"Ms. Asche."

Blondie relayed the information then turned to us. "Please, follow me." She led us through a small labyrinth of cubicles until we entered a quiet inner office. Another receptionist sat at a grandiose desk.

This receptionist could be my grandmother, and with one smile, she gave the impression of trustworthiness. "It's a pleasure to meet you, Ms. Asche. Mr. Kohl briefed me on your case this morning, and of course, I met—"

Arch stepped out of his office then. "Hey, guys! Come on in! Ellie, you look well." *He noticed the changes. Crap, it wasn't subtle enough.* I sent Todd a death glare over my shoulder.

We followed Arch into his office. He pointed to a posh seating area in one corner. "I *am* well, thanks." I started to sit beside Todd on a leather couch, Arch's fancy diploma hanging on the wall, framed with a picture, distracted me.

I walked over to get a better view. A younger Arch stood with two men and a woman in the picture. "Your family?" He nodded. I read his diploma, caught up by his name, printed in script. "Archibald Duke Beaumont?" I pointed at his name. "Is this for real?"

Arch sighed. "Yes," he said with an embarrassed voice. "Can we get down to business?" I laughed and agreed so he'd continue. "I've got the contract here. As discussed, our partners, Adrian Kohl and Marcus Stedmon will take your case. They should be here any moment. We've delegated their other cases to junior partners in the firm."

"I don't mean to impose. Is my case going to be difficult?"

"Not difficult, necessarily, but there will be leg work involved. And we don't take on a lot of cases over the holidays if we can help it. This works out nicely for everyone. We're happy to accept your case."

He pulled a stack of paperwork out of the file. "This is

a standard contract. It covers their time, fees, and work they'll do for you. I encourage you to take it home, read it in full." He slid the small pile of papers into the folder. "Maybe have Charles take a gander at it. When you're satisfied, sign it and include the first retainer."

He showed us all of his teeth in a winning smile, and Todd took in a small breath. "Dear lord," he whispered, barely audible.

"What was that?" Arch asked.

"Nothing, clearing my throat," Todd replied. As a giggle escaped me, the door opened, and Gray and Wes walked in.

"Sweet mother of all, it's a trifecta of...I don't even have a word for it." I didn't think Todd meant for me to hear him, but that didn't stop my giggling. It was the first time he'd seen Wes and Gray, though he'd heard plenty from me.

"Hi, guys!" I said after I took a moment to mask the laughter in my voice.

"Hey, Ellie," said Wes. He wore a dark blue polo. His biceps strained the material of the sleeves.

"What's so funny?" asked Gray. He also wore a polo, burnt orange. His biceps weren't stressing his shirt quite as much as Wes's, but plenty distracted the eye. His loose hair cascaded down his back.

"Todd made a, uh, funny noise. Inside joke," I replied lamely. "Arch has been explaining everything to me. I appreciate you guys taking me on."

"Hey, it's no problem," replied Wes.

"Ellie, forgive the personal question, but how are you set on money? They will, of course, need access to all of your accounting records, but is there an immediate need for them to unfreeze any assets?" asked Gray.

"You're sweet for asking, but I was given my trust fund when I turned eighteen. I don't think I could spend all of the money my father gave me if I tried. A large portion of it is tied up in investments, of course, but I'm fine. I don't need the income from the company, and that's not why I'm doing this." I didn't care about the money from the company. I cared about the legacy.

We stood to leave. "Wes, Gray, this is my best friend Todd. Todd, meet Wes and Gray." Todd gave the guys a bit of a sizing-up glance, then strode forward to shake their hands.

"It's nice to meet you both," Todd said in a deep voice. "I'm sure we will see more of each other soon."

Wes grinned at me over Todd's head. "Any friend of Ellie's, and all that."

We followed Wes and Gray out and they took off for destinations unknown. Before I shut the door to his office, Arch stopped me. "Wait, Ellie."

I turned. "Yes, Arch?"

"Could we have dinner sometime?" He rubbed his neck and glanced down, like a teenager asking a girl out for the first time. My eyebrows flew up. "I mean, it can be as friends!" He blurted out, amending his original sentence.

"Yeah, sure. We could hang out sometime. Just call or text me. You've got my number." I turned and walked out of the office before I could melt into a puddle on the swanky office floor.

The kindly receptionist led Todd and me to a conference room to meet the other partners. Mr. Stedmon and Mr. Kohl were older, jovial men, perhaps in their mid-fifties. They showed signs of middle-of-life spread but seemed happy for it. Our meeting was a positive one. I gave them every detail about my stepmother I could think of, with several interjections from Todd.

"Miss Ellie, don't worry. We're good at what we do. I'm convinced it won't take much to show a judge you deserve to follow in your father's footsteps, according to his wishes."

"Thank you. You eased my mind tremendously. Please, contact me anytime if I can help with the case." They assured me since the next meeting was a further informal hearing with the judge I wouldn't be bothered much by them; it would be all on their plates.

It wouldn't be until we went to trial that I'd begin to spend a lot of time being prepped and coached to be effective in front of the jury. I shook both of their hands, and we made our exit.

Once outside their office, I grabbed Todd's arm. "Let's *go*. Now. I've been dying to tell you what happened." I hadn't had a chance to tell him Arch asked me out.

He gave me a startled glance as I swept us past the sweet receptionist, through the cubicles, and out to the front office. He turned and gave a finger wave to Blondie as I practically ran us out.

Once we reached the quiet of the empty elevator, I collapsed against him. "I just got asked out on a date by Arch Beaumont. And he was *nervous about it.*"

Todd's mouth dropped open. "Dear lord, forget shopping for me. It's fairy godmother time."

CHAPTER FIVE

Too many bodies and too much noise permeated the mall. Todd ran around in rare form, excited to send me off on a date with the gorgeous lawyer. He dragged me from store to store, buying enough clothing to send me on fourteen dates and him on another three. We were both overloaded with bags and making our way to the exit when one of my nightmares walked toward me—my stepsister. Halfway across the mall, the derision on her face came into focus as she made a beeline for us.

Todd nearly dropped his bags when he spotted her. "Oh, god, where can we hide? I don't have the energy for that bitch after all the shopping we did."

"Neither do I." The back of my neck clenched painfully. I rolled my head to ward off the oncoming tension.

"At least you look killer today. Hold your head high;

you're ten times the woman she is, inside and out." His words gave me the strength to shake my hair out and stick my nose in the air as she reached us.

"Hello, Michelle." The frown on my face came out in my voice.

"Ellie. What're you doing here? You don't shop." Her snide voice infuriated me.

"You have no idea what I do or don't do." I tried to keep my voice even, showing no sign of upset.

She sneered at the various bags we carried. "Trying to burn through your meager trust fund?" She laughed. "I'd think you'd learn to be more frugal since you won't have any income from the company." Taking her cue from her mother, she always belittled me as a kid. I refused to let her bother me now. I'd no longer let her shake my self-confidence. I wasn't a chubby teen anymore.

I arched an eyebrow but otherwise gave no expression, intentionally keeping my face blank. With all the grace as I could muster, I calmly replied, "You can believe what you'd like, Michelle. We'll sort it out in court. Now, excuse us, please. Have a good day." I attempted to sidestep her, but she blocked my path.

"No amount of expensive clothes will make you desirable, Ellie." Her predictable words weren't even the worst she typically offered.

"Michelle, maybe you should eat some makeup so you'll be pretty on the inside," Todd cut in. He'd been quiet as long as he could stand, knowing I'd want to fight the battle my way. She refused to even glance Todd's way, tossed her hair and took off.

"Do you have any idea how hard it was for me to be silent? I'm sorry, but I had to," Todd's words rang empty. He wasn't sorry, but I didn't blame him one bit.

"It's okay, I'm not mad." I tried to grab his hand, but couldn't reach it under all the bags.

We ended up following Michelle toward the exit. She turned off into a shop near the door. "Look at that outfit! She has no clue how to dress for her body type, and she says *you're* not desirable. What a horrible little woman!" Todd's rant made me giggle.

"Yes, she is. But we'll stomp her mom in court, and she'll have nothing she can possibly say." *God, I hope I'm right.* Todd held the door open for me to walk into the parking garage. We loaded the car quietly and left.

Todd pulled out of the mall parking lot into traffic. "When's the date?"

"He didn't specify. He said sometime." I sighed and watched traffic pass us while we waited to turn onto the interstate ramp. "I don't know, did I exaggerate his asking? Maybe he did want to hang out as friends."

"You said he seemed flustered. You were pretty sure at the time that he wanted an actual date."

"Yeah, that's true. We'll see if he ever goes through with setting a date and time." Todd took us to a burger joint near our apartment building to get dinner for us and Rick. We spent the evening watching an old army show on Netflix and munching on french fries. Todd spent part of the evening hanging up all of our purchases. Rick and I tried to help, but he wouldn't let us. He swore it was his favorite part.

With no real holiday plans, I slept in the next morning. I awoke to two missed text messages.

Wes: I enjoyed seeing you yesterday. It was too brief. Coffee one day soon?

Heat flooded my stomach. Though excited to get a message from Wes, I checked the other text before replying.

Arch: Dinner Friday night? I got theater tickets.

I replied to Arch, and we agreed I'd be ready at six.

I sent a text to Todd letting him know. His reply was immediate.

Todd: Dammit! It's Black Friday. No way am I shopping in that. We'll make do.

I laughed. He'd figure it out. No way would I go back to the mall. I switched to the text with Wes.

Ellie: Sure, sounds good. When?

His reply came later while I munched on a bowl of cereal. I hoped he'd gotten busy with family Thanksgiving stuff and hadn't forgotten me.

Wes: Sorry for the delay. Saturday? I'm free after two.

I didn't know where my surge of confidence came from—two different dates, two days in a row—but I liked it. I bit my lip in excitement and typed out my reply.

Ellie: Works for me. See you at the coffee shop by your office at two.

By the time Todd let himself into my apartment

Friday, I was pacing the floor. Satan sat on my bed, glaring at me as I moved. I'd already gone through the plucking, lotioning, and exfoliating regimen he taught me days before. My hair was in a towel, and my face was ready for Todd's expertise.

"Hurry! My hair is going to dry. I got excited and showered too early."

Todd scurried over and took the bottle of hair product I offered. "My word, you're a nervous wreck. Sit down and let me fix you up. I'm going to give you a glossier hairdo this time, as you'll be at the theater. You've got to dress up for this."

"I hadn't even thought of that! Do I have a dress?" My nerves were a wreck. At that moment, I would've done anything Todd told me to, including shopping.

"Of course you do! What do you take me for?" He laughed as he massaged the goop into my hair.

Todd took his time and made my hair and makeup dramatic for my date. He called it an evening look. Finally, he finished, and I checked out his completed work. He gave me a smoky eye and bold lip, tamed my hair into a sleek side sweep. My blond tresses had never been shinier. "I still feel like the same person, just… nice. Pretty"

"That's because I'm that good, darling. And you have fantastic hair." He held out my dress for me to step into. The theater didn't call for full formal—he'd made me text Arch and find out where we were going so he'd know how to dress me. I ended up in a sleeveless, black, sparkly cocktail dress with a sultry diagonal hemline.

"You're perfection. My job is done. Call me after." With an air kiss, he left. Five minutes later, my doorbell rang. I checked the monitors to find Arch standing in the hall in a form fitting suit.

I let him in, and like a hero in a novel, he nearly took my breath away. His hair had a small spike in the front, which elongated his features. I could tell he'd shaved, but he already showed the smallest signs of stubble. *Sexy as all hell.*

"Hi," I said, voice small.

"You look amazing." Arch's eyes raked up and down my body, making me shiver. My spine straightened under his gaze.

"Thank you. You look stunning yourself." I felt like a fool complimenting a man like him, but he cut a hell of a figure.

"Did you have a nice Thanksgiving?" His eyes bored into mine.

"It was fine." I'd spent the day with Todd and Rick. I couldn't do a big Thanksgiving without my dad. "How was yours?"

He gave me an odd glance at the word fine but nodded his head. "Good. I spent it with the guys and my little sister, Moriah. Most of our family is all in Atlanta, so we usually have a dinner at Gray's place."

I grinned up at him while he continued rattling off his Thanksgiving day story. He seemed a little off kilter. I flattered myself to hope he was as nervous as I was. "Should we go?" I asked when he trailed off his speech about well-prepared turkey.

He motioned me to the exit, and I led the way. Once I locked up, I asked the question on my mind for days. "So, you didn't want to talk about the case then?"

He had the decency to duck his head in shame. "No, not at all. To keep things ethical, we can't discuss anything else about your case anymore."

I laughed nervously. I didn't want to have to worry about an ethics violation for my case. "Are you sure it's okay for us to do this?"

"Absolutely. I'm not your lawyer, and as long as I give you no legal advice and don't work on your case, we're good to go. Your case isn't in my expertise."

Relief flooded me. "All right then. Let's go."

We walked down to the parking garage, and he opened my door in a show of chivalry. "After you, my lady," he said with a deep bow.

"Thank you, kind sir!" I replied with an exaggerated southern belle accent.

I settled in the leather seat and strapped in while he walked around to the driver's side. For the life of me, I couldn't imagine what to say to the gorgeous man sitting beside me as he pulled out of the parking garage into the dreary evening rain.

"Have you seen this production before?" Arch asked as he merged into traffic. Rain splattered the windshield in a soothing pattern.

"No, but I've always wanted to. My father and I used to go to the theater often, but somehow always missed this one. He was a little afraid of cats, and I'm told they're heavily featured."

The booming laughter he let out startled me. I hadn't meant to be funny, more sarcastic. "You're hilarious, Ellie. Where'd you get your sense of humor?"

"My mom," I said with a smile, glad I entertained him. "We always told her she could've been a *comedienne*." In the middle of telling him her favorite joke about a priest and a rabbi, a rapid motion outside my window caught my eye. Before I realized what the motion meant, a large vehicle veered out of the other lane and sideswiped our SUV. My head knocked into the passenger window hard enough to make me see stars as the airbags on my side of the car narrowly missed my face.

Arch struggled to regain control of the car as it slipped on the wet street. I turned my fuzzy head to the right to find a large Dooley truck still pushing the SUV across the median and into the path of oncoming traffic. The driver of the truck appeared to be unconscious. Despite my crushing headache, I managed to yell out, "*Arch!* Floor it! You've got to get in front of this truck before he kills us." I tried not to scream the words. Staying calm seemed a better idea than panicking.

To his credit, he trusted me enough to not question my words. He got a hold of himself and stomped the gas. He jumped the SUV forward and to the right side of the road but then slammed on the brakes, as he successfully avoided plowing into a sedan in front of us. More tires squealed behind us, and another large crash jerked us forward and back again. Next to me, Arch's airbags exploded.

I stared stupidly at my seat belt buckle. My fingers wouldn't work properly to unlatch it. Arch leaned forward with his head on the steering wheel. "Are you okay?" I asked, terrified he wouldn't be able to answer.

"Yes, trying to get my head to stop swimming." His voice sounded far away. "And wondering why your side airbags didn't go off."

My seat belt eventually unlatched. "I'm going to go check if the other driver is hurt. You stay there, you're bleeding." Blood trickled out of his nose.

"I'm coming, too, babe. I'll be fine, and I'm not the only one bleeding." He reached up and stroked the side of my head and then showed me the blood on his fingers.

"I must be in shock or something. I couldn't feel your fingers touching my head." My hearing was still a little off, almost like a ringing sound. "I'm sure someone already called 911. Let's go check on him." Arch nodded, airbag burns already prominent on his face.

I tried to open my door, but it was jammed shut. "You get out, and I'll slide over there. This side is too badly damaged." My entire body shook from the shock.

Arch climbed out, and his bloody hand reached in to help me move over to the driver's side. I could've done it on my own, but I appreciated him offering the help. My knees quaked once I stood on the road outside. My wobbly legs didn't appreciate the heels. I lifted my face skyward, thankful for the rain, cooling my adrenaline-heated skin and washing away the blood.

We made our way over to the truck. The hood was crumpled, while the bumper on the truck lifted the rear of our SUV. People swarmed the wreck while we oriented ourselves.

Arch approached one of the men as he walked away from the truck. "Is he okay?"

The man raised his eyebrows at our appearance and injuries. "A lot worse off than you two. We started to come check on you but saw you both moving around. He needed attention first. Turns out it wasn't all that needed." The man removed his cap. "He's gone."

"He's dead?" I asked, incredulous.

"Yeah, but he doesn't have any visible wounds. We think maybe he had a heart attack or stroke or something and that's what caused him to wreck into you two. How are you both? You look like you need to sit down."

"We need to be checked out," Arch replied. "But we'll live. Are you sure he's gone? Did anyone try CPR?"

"Yeah, that lady over there." He pointed to a well-dressed woman still leaning into the truck. "She said he was gone. Said she's a nurse."

Sirens cut through the sound of rain hitting the pavement. Adrenaline stopped coursing through my body, and my limbs began to shake again. My skin rapidly became chilled, and the rain started to stab my bare shoulders and arms like violent little icicles. A jacket was placed around me, and I looked up, head swimming, to Arch positioning it to protect my skin from the drizzle. I leaned into him for a comforting hug, thankful to be alive.

When the ambulance pulled up, we motioned it to the truck, in hopes the woman was mistaken. A second ambulance pulled up behind it, along with two police cars and a fire truck. Concerned emergency workers soon swamped us.

A paramedic told me to move my eyes this way and that while he shined a light. Arch was being put through the same routine out of my line of sight. Once deemed fit to travel, they ushered us into an ambulance together.

The driver of the truck was definitely deceased and, to my relief, given the other ambulance to himself. My heart hurt for him and his family, especially having so recently lost a loved one, but I couldn't stomach the concept of riding in an ambulance with a dead person.

I'd never ridden in an ambulance before, and the experience unsettled me. I didn't like riding backward, but Arch insisted I ride on the stretcher. He sat on the bench beside me and held my hand while the paramedics did what they could with our injuries.

"My father died of a pulmonary embolism," I said, voice hushed. The paramedic glanced from Arch to me and moved to sit up front with the driver since he'd finished the first aid. "If he'd been driving when it happened, this would've happened to him. It was so fast, there was no time to react or save him." I expected a hot, searing pain to hit my heart with the words but felt only a dull throb. I was beginning to heal.

Arch clasped my hand. "I'm so sorry. Were you with

him?"

"No, and part of me is glad, and part is sad." Arch began to stroke my forearm with a light touch, showing he was there for me, even if he didn't have words to comfort me. "If I'd been with him, I would've had to *see* the light leave his eyes. I don't know if I could've handled it." The pain in my heart throbbed a little harder. "But on the other hand, if I'd been there, maybe I would've noticed something sooner and gotten help."

"Where did it happen?" I closed my eyes, the memories of the awful day causing my stomach to churn more than it already was.

"At the office. He was in a meeting with his assistant, Claire, and one of his favorite editors, Rebecca. They told me he was gone before they even finished dialing 911."

"If he went so quickly, then there would've been nothing you could've done. It sounds like it only took a few minutes to take his life." His eyes, more brown than green for the moment, were filled with tears.

"My head knows that, but it's hard to tell my heart." I rested my head on the bed and clasped his hand. He sensed my need for quiet, and we spent the rest of the ride in silence. It was companionable and not at all uncomfortable. I tried to push visions of the day my father died out of my taxed brain, but I became plagued with the scenes of his funeral passing behind my closed eyelids.

The glossy black wood of the casket reflected the spring sunlight and hurt my eyes. I couldn't look away. The pain in my eyes was nothing compared to the breathtaking agony in my chest. Thinking about the pain made it worse. My breath shortened while my sternum was being crushed by my grief. My ears rang. A voice kept talking and talking, but it was tinny and far-off. A minister, it was a minister. A minister, because I was at a funeral for my dad.

In that box was the last of my family. My father was... Daddy, how did this happen? I gripped my knees to combat the pain, digging my nails in until it hurt. I finally tore my eyes away from the wood containing my father to stare at the drop of blood my nails brought out of my skin.

I blinked at them once, twice, while the droning of a faceless minister irritated my ears. My leg was cut. How did that happen? Fingers wrapped around my hand, gently pulling it away from my knee. I looked up at Todd, my best friend in the world, my rock. His eyes swam with tears. He whispered something to me and squeezed my hand, but my ears wouldn't work right.

I looked to the casket, focusing on the man in clergy robes speaking behind it. Why was he speaking? I'd never seen him before in my life. I turned to Todd. "Why is he here?" Todd shushed me. "Why... I don't understand what's going on." I trailed off in a whisper. "Why is he dead?"

Todd pulled me into an embrace to shush me. My body was limp, so I leaned against him. Everything was wrong, wrong with the world, wrong. Wrong, this is wrong. Why are we here? I watched the sunlight on the casket again, but black began to crowd my vision. Wrong, wrong, wrong. My heart beat in unison with my obsessive thoughts. Wrong.

"Breathe, Ellie. You're going to pass out." A voice with hot breath whispered in my ear, startling me and causing me to suck in a deep breath. Spots dotted around my eyes, and I understood the world

again. The world was cruel, and my father was dead.

I turned to my right, to the hot-breathed voice, the man that swept my Todd off his feet. Rick. He married Todd, and I was thrilled with the match because he was so good for Todd. He was good for Todd.

Todd would get me through this pain. Todd would help me. Todd always helped me. He helped me when my mom died. He helped me when my father remarried, and I realized what a witch my stepmother was. I remembered then that my stepmother was there. She was there, and so were her offspring.

She sat in a black suit, her red hair glistening in the sun. She looked beautiful, regal. Pitifully, she dabbed her eyes behind her round black sunglasses with a pristine white handkerchief. My upper lip curled. She had the face of an angel, but her heart was black and evil. I knew that firsthand.

The sun flashed off the wood, again, and I jerked my gaze to my father. My father. He taught me so much. He taught me how to be kind. He taught me how to persevere. He taught me how to do algebra when I couldn't get the concept. He taught me how to swim.

A soprano voice, singing a song I'd never heard snapped me out of my memories. I sucked in another breath and regretted the interruption. For a moment, the pain lessened as I remembered my parents when we were happiest, the summer before Mom was diagnosed. I caught lightning bugs at dusk while my parents fed each other roasted marshmallows.

The soprano finally stopped her warbling, and my father's best friend, Charles, stood. His words didn't penetrate the fog in my brain, either. I went back to gazing at the box that would finally take my father from me for good. To be a thing of torture, it was pretty.

My chest constricted again. "Breathe," Todd whispered, his head above mine. I realized he was still holding me tight. I pulled away and straightened in my chair, directly in front of the offending box.

"I'm twenty-years, seven months, and thirteen days old," I whispered. It seemed important to remember that. I needed to know how many days I had with my father. Twenty-years, seven months, and thirteen days, and then I put him in a box and put that box in the ground. My chest hurt so much. It stabbed.

"What was that, dear?" I blinked at Charles, once, twice, but didn't answer him. He was talking directly to me, now. I couldn't remember when he'd moved from behind the casket to stand so close to me. I couldn't see my father because Charles blocked my view.

Whatever else he said, I nodded, and he walked away. I didn't mean to be rude; he was a wonderful man and a lifelong friend to my father. I simply couldn't hear him.

Nobody took Charles's place to speak about the man I loved so dearly. The man that was healthy only one week before. Wrong. It was so wrong. Todd pulled me to my feet as people began to file in front of me, grabbing my hand and shaking it.

"Thank you," I murmured to another person I couldn't see or hear. I hoped I was saying the right things, but my body was on autopilot. My eyes stayed glued to the casket until the next person blocked my view and I was forced to say some sort of appreciation for their condolences. When I could think clearly again, I'd have Todd tell me who I spoke to and what they said. I knew I'd appreciate it one day, but on that day, I couldn't hear them. Why was the world so wrong?

Luckily for my stomach, the ride, even without the

lights and sirens, passed quickly. I guessed our injuries weren't threatening enough to warrant all the hoopla, and I was thankful for it. The press would make enough of a commotion when they found out.

Arch sent Gray and Wes a text before the ambulance left the scene of the crash. They somehow managed to beat us to the hospital and waited for us in the ambulance bay. Gray's skin was pale with worry. Wes continuously wrapped the shaggy strands of his hair nervously around his fingers. Their concern for their best friend made me smile.

Gray and Wes ran over to check on Arch as the paramedics helped him out of the rig. As soon as my gurney was wheeled out of the truck, they abandoned Arch to stand on either side of me. As the paramedic pushed me into the ER, Arch trudged behind us until the other paramedic rushed over to him with a wheelchair.

We moved as a group into a large room with two beds and curtains for privacy. Wes opened the curtains as the nurses helped settle us into the beds. People in scrubs and white coats scurried around us both, hooking us up to monitors to take our heart rates and blood pressures. They asked us a million questions about what happened, where it hurt, and our medical histories. Lights were shined in our eyes, muscles were squeezed, and heads were examined thoroughly. Finally, the medical experts did enough preliminary work to leave us in peace while they ordered CAT scans.

"What the hell. You two don't look that bad, but

they're treating you like you've got broken necks." Gray, visibly agitated, darted his eyes around the room nervously.

"Are you all right?" I asked.

"I'm not a big fan of hospitals. They make me nervous."

"We will be fine, man. I need my nose set and, at worst, she probably needs a few stitches." Arch turned to me with a lowered voice. "When we were kids, he had a bad experience in a hospital." I turned to Gray sympathetically.

"I know that, but my heart is racing. Ignore me. I won't be able to calm down until we're out of this place." He sat in the corner and darted his eyes around while he took deep calming breaths.

Wes sat on a small rolling stool and wheeled over to me, feet up, like a child playing at a doctor's appointment. "I'm going to sleep on your couch tonight, little Ellie. And Gray can sleep on Arch's. That way if either of you need anything, you've got us."

"That's sweet, but I'm sure I'll be fine. I doubt I even need stitches." My head pounded as I said it. *Maybe I'll need stitches after all.*

"I insist. You're not going to lift a finger after this idiot almost got you killed." He pointed to a bruised Arch. The skin around his eyes was a deep purple.

"I didn't almost get her killed! That guy had a heart attack or something." Arch's voice was a mix of pissed and panicked that someone would assume he hurt me.

"I'm messing with you, man. We all know you didn't

do it on purpose. These things happen." Wes wheeled over to squeeze his friend's arm and show he didn't mean his teasing words.

A nurse walked in with two charts, followed by an orderly. "All right, dearies, it's time for the CAT scan. Then you'll come back here to wait for the results."

She turned to the guys. "Gentlemen, this could take a while. Would you prefer to wait here or go out until they return?"

Gray and Wes looked at each other for a moment, then turned to Arch. "We're going to go get some dinner. Text us when you're back in here, and we'll come quick."

"Sounds good, man, thanks," Arch and Wes did some sort of complicated handshake, then Gray gave Arch a high five. Then, the two hotties came over to my bed. Each grabbed one of my hands and simultaneously brought them to their lips. With their lips on my hands, lava worked its way down my body as they stared at me through their eyelashes.

I believed they meant it as a gentlemanly and flirty gesture, but it was incredibly sensual. My mind strayed. *Dear lord, now I want to know what else they might be able to do as a team… Ellie, don't be a dirty whore. You've only known them a few days.* "Bye, guys," I whispered. With a bow and a flourish, they left.

I giggled and turned to Arch. "You have some competition, Romeo."

Arch laughed at my expression and raised his eyebrows. "I'm not worried."

The nurse interrupted our banter to take us to our test. The CAT scan waiting room was lined with beds and wheelchairs filled with injured people. Arch distracted me from the waiting and my growing headache by telling me about his little sister, Moriah, who he was close to growing up. His parents lived in Atlanta, but he wasn't as close with them.

When his head started hurting, too, I told him about my mom and dad. I spoke softly, reflecting on the joyous time before Mom's death and especially before the stepbitch came into the picture.

My head nestled comfortably on the pillow, and I only meant to close my eyes for a moment. The next thing I knew, a nurse wheeled me into a small room with a large circular machine in it. I drifted off again once settled in for the scan and didn't wake up until we were in the ER. I didn't remember getting out of the machine and onto the bed. Arch talked to Wes and Gray quietly from the bed beside me.

"I'm sorry, guys. I didn't mean to sleep through your visit. I hope I didn't snore!" I checked for drool and found a nice wet spot on my pillow. When random shouting in the hall distracted the three of them, I flipped my pillow over to hide the moisture.

"Don't worry, Ellie." Gray came over and stroked my hair out of my face. "You're given a pass to sleep as long as someone watches you. Plus, after your CAT scan, they gave you a shot in the arm. You woke up, but it worked fast. You conked out."

"What did they give me? How long was I out?" I hated missing time.

"She said it was a painkiller and anti-nausea medicine combined. And about two hours. We should be close to being discharged." Arch stared at me around a big white bandage on his face. The bruises around his eyes darkened in the time I slept. "You talk in your sleep."

"I'm a vivid dreamer." I didn't want to talk about the types of dreams I had. The worst of them were related to my family. I tried to take the focus off of myself. "You look pitiful. Is your nose broken?"

Arch shook his head. "No, but it's pretty banged up. It should heal a lot faster than a break, thankfully. And burns from the airbags and whiplash. I've got to take it easy for a few days. You've got a mild concussion and need to be monitored through the night for regular breathing. We told the nurse that Gray is your fiancé. They gave him all the discharge instructions." I gazed from Arch to Gray as Arch continued, "I was going to say it was me, but Gray beat me to it."

Wes's laugh filled the room. "I was going to, as well."

"I don't think I can have three fiancées, but whatever floats your boats!" I watched the boys give a few subtle glances between themselves but chalked it up to my concussion.

The nurse returned and gave me my discharge instructions, which matched what I'd already been told. Wes snatched the prescriptions for pain and nausea medicines from the nurse so I wouldn't have to deal with it. "I'll get these filled on the way home. Hand me your insurance card and tell me where to go."

I wrote down my usual pharmacy on the corner of the discharge instructions and handed it over. It happened to be the same one Arch used. He gave Wes his prescriptions.

When I tried to move unassisted from the bed to the wheelchair, dizziness almost put me on the ground. Gray caught me and propped me up against him before I could ask for help. He practically carried me to the wheelchair, and then took up a post behind me. He was overly concerned for a man I'd only met once at a party. His attitude was sincere, though. I let him fuss. I suspected some of his motivation came from his childhood trauma about hospitals.

The nurse gave me a knowing grin and busied herself behind Arch before Wes shooed her away. She led the way to the patient loading area where Gray's black SUV—remarkably like Arch's—was waiting.

"Do you guys buy them in bulk?" I asked sarcastically.

Arch laughed and shook his head. "No, Gray got one first, and I liked it so much I bought one, too."

Gray helped me into the front. Arch toughed it out and helped himself into the back seat while Wes chuckled. "I could've helped you in, Arch."

"I'm a big boy," Arch said with a grumpy frown. Wes rolled his eyes.

"I'll meet you at your apartments after I get your medicine," Wes said. He turned toward the parking lot to get his truck and go to the pharmacy.

I drifted off again on the ride home. I didn't expect I'd be comfortable sitting in the same type car we'd wrecked, but Gray and Arch gave me a sense of safety. Plus, I knew Gray was especially on edge and took extra precautions. We pulled into my parking garage, and Gray rushed over to help me. He offered his hand as I stepped out of the SUV and immediately began to teeter.

I wasn't dizzy; I teetered because I still wore the damn heels. I refrained from cursing Todd; he couldn't have foreseen such a need-to-wear-flats situation. Gray responded immediately. He scooped me into his arms so swiftly the garage spun. I rested my head against his shoulder and enjoyed the ride, once again grateful we had access to the parking garage. The press outside the front door would have a field day with pictures of Gray carrying me in the building.

Once home, I changed into comfy pants and an oversized tee, relieved to take the fancy dress off. Gray insisted I settle into bed. He propped me up with pillows, left my phone and the TV remote beside me, and left to check on Arch. My eyes closed and I fell asleep before he left my apartment.

CHAPTER SIX

My neck cramped, and my body overheated under the thick comforter. I didn't understand why it covered me, as I usually removed it from the bed and only used a light quilt. The flat screen mounted on the wall gave the only light in the room. Satan purred, curled up at my chest.

My throat cried for water, and my bladder cried to be emptied. All in all, I was groggy, confused, and in pain. I scooted my way over to the edge of the bed and slipped my feet out of the blankets. It took me a minute to stand and trudge over to my bathroom. Finally, the dizziness passed. As long as I moved slowly, I stayed steady.

Part of the reason for my sweating was the flannel pajama pants I wore. I slept in a tee and undies. I pushed the miserably hot pants to my ankles and stepped out of them.

Next problem—my dry mouth. Shuffling my feet on

the thick carpet, I made my way across my living room to the kitchen to get a glass of ice cold milk. I set the glass on the counter a little forcefully. My arms didn't work quite like they should. I tried to handle the full gallon of milk but ended up slamming it on the counter as well, too disoriented to manage its weight.

A hand on my waist made me jump, and the scream that left my lips would've given Todd a run for his money. I twirled around to find Wes standing behind me with a shocked expression on his face. Pain and dizziness overwhelmed me, and I grabbed the counter to steady myself. "I didn't know you were still here!"

Wes's hand on my waist tightened. He put his other hand on my shoulder to give me a little support. "I told you I was sleeping on your couch. I wasn't kidding." He pulled a small bottle of pills out of his pocket. "Here, take one with your milk. Are you hungry? I could make you a grilled cheese or something."

My stomach protested the idea of food. "No, I don't think I could eat now. I'll drink the milk, it should be enough." I downed the pill with the milk Wes poured for me. Icy heaven slid down my throat, cooling me off.

When I set the empty glass in the sink, I leaned against the counter and felt the cool wood of the lower cabinets on my thighs. *I don't have pants on.* My t-shirt barely covered my private areas. A blush stained my cheeks. "Thanks, I'm going to bed!" I spat out, my voice high-pitched and tinny.

"I'll walk you." Wes took my elbow. All I could focus on was my bare legs. *It's no different than what he'd see at the pool!* Somehow, pale pink panties and my bathing suit bottoms were two totally different beasts.

In my room, I started to drag my comforter off my bed until I realized my bottom would be exposed. "Wes? Would you mind pulling the thick comforter off my bed? It makes me too warm at night."

As soon as he finished straightening the bed, I crowded him until he was out the door, shutting it behind him. My eyelids suddenly wanted to close, thanks to the powerful little pill. I looked forward to the pending oblivion. "Thank you for the help. I'll yell if I need anything," I called through the door. Before I crawled under the covers, I stumbled to my chest of drawers and found a pair of boxers to wear under my t-shirt. At least I'd be decent if I got up again.

The next thing I knew, light blazed through my windows, and Wes bent over me, staring at me like a puzzle to solve. My eyes widened as I fought to stifle yet another scream. He *had* to stop scaring me. "What're you doing?" I croaked, a little surprised he let himself into in my bedroom uninvited. I didn't know why it surprised me, though, since he already spent the night in my apartment.

The side of the bed sank with Wes's weight as he sat beside me. "The nurse told me to check on your breathing. I've been in here every two hours all night." I stared at him in shock, mouth open. I'd no clue. A high school band could've played a set in my bedroom, and I would've slept through it. "Plus, you talked in your sleep again, and I stayed a minute to try to figure out what you were saying," he said unashamedly.

"Did you figure anything out?" I hoped he hadn't.

"You said something about Mitch. Who's that?" He stroked my hair and checked me over carefully. I'd no intention of telling him anything about my stepbrother then.

"Someone I knew growing up. What time is it?" I sat up and rubbed my sore head.

"Ten. Arch and Gray have already been over a few times, and your friend from downstairs started trying to reach you at seven. He's pretty mad at you for not calling him. You'd better be prepared." My stomach sank. It never occurred to me to call Todd. I bet he was furious. I'd be furious if he got in a wreck and didn't call me. I grabbed my phone to find seventeen missed calls and about forty texts, all from Todd.

"My phone doesn't seem to be on vibrate, but I didn't hear it ring. I wonder if it got damaged in the wreck." I contemplated the boredom of going to the cell phone store for a repair and decided to buy a new phone. I'd get Todd one as a present to help apologize for my blunder.

"Call him." He tapped my phone. "I promised him you would as soon as you woke up."

"I'll call him in two minutes." I pushed Wes off the bed and got up to use the bathroom. As soon as I finished, I peeked out of my room to find Wes moving around my kitchen. I collapsed onto the bed, grabbed my phone, and hit my speed dial.

"*What's* going on? Are you okay? I've been worried

sick." Todd's voice came shrilly out of the phone. I pulled it away from my ear before he made my headache worse.

"Todd, I'm so sorry. I'm the worst friend ever." I dropped my head into my free hand, ashamed of myself.

"I thought you'd been ax murdered!" He sounded close to tears.

I winced and rubbed my head. His voice rang too loud for my headache. "I was confused and disoriented, and the guys took care of everything. I didn't think to call."

"That's crap!" I grimaced again and turned the volume the rest of the way down. "You always call me, unless you do need help, then you take everything on yourself and try not to bother me. When're you going to learn? I want to be there for the good *and* the bad!"

"I'm sorry, so sorry, Todd. You know I love you, and you're my best friend in the whole world. I'll make this up to you." A cell phone wouldn't be enough. I'd have to grovel. I hated how much he worried.

"Damn right you will, missy!" His voice softened. "Now, are you okay or not?"

"I think so. I'm banged up and sore. I have a mild concussion, that's throwing me a little. Overall though, it could've been a lot worse." I curled onto my side, tired.

"Do you need anything?"

"No, Arch feels guilty I was with him when this happened, and the three of them haven't let me lift a finger."

"Good. Let them. They almost got you killed. I'd like to concuss all of them!" I could picture him waving his fist as he spoke.

I laughed. "I don't think to concuss is a thing."

"I'll make it a thing. I'm that mad."

"There's no way Arch could've avoided this, Todd. Don't be mad. And if they keep spoiling me like this, well, hell, I could get used to it." I wouldn't complain about the spoiling part, only the pain.

"I'll be up in an hour-ish to check on you. I love you." His sad voice hit me right in the guilt. I really hurt him.

"I love you, too, and again, I'm sorry I didn't call you." Tears fell down my cheeks. I hated causing him any sliver of pain, especially considering how he spoiled me.

"I forgive you if you promise to call if you need anything at all. Even if you only need someone to lift the remote and change the channel for you. Call me!"

"I promise. I promise with sugar on top."

"Okay. Bye."

I tried to decide what to do next—wallow in my guilt until I fell asleep or go forage for food. Mouth-watering smells soon drifted into my bedroom. Searching for food won.

I still wore the boxers from my middle of the night embarrassment, but I made a stop in the bathroom to splash water on my face and brush my hair. I didn't want to look *too* dragon lady-ish and scare him away completely.

I walked out to find Wes gone and Gray cooking in my kitchen. "Good morning," I said.

"Morning. Sorry for the intrusion, but I make a better breakfast than Wes does." I laughed at their switcharoo.

Bacon sizzled in a pan, and biscuits rose in the oven. He even put butter out to soften. I helped myself to a glass of orange juice and sat on one of the bar stools across from the cook top to wait for my breakfast to be finished.

"You practice law *and* cook? What else can you do?" I winked, feeling much more flirtatious than normal. His head rose from the pan with a mixed expression of desire and incredulity. He liked me teasing him. After his care at the hospital, it was good to tease him a bit.

"I love to cook. So you know, I can make things more complicated than a simple southern breakfast," he replied as he stirred gravy for the biscuits. I caught him tossing Satan bits of bacon out of the corner of my eye.

"Oh? You'll have to try to impress me one day. I love to cook, as well." I could make a handful of dishes, and the rest? Follow the recipe and pray.

"I'd be glad to if you'll return the favor."

I grinned into my orange juice. I'd made another date with one of my hunky lawyers. It was some sort of record. I couldn't wait to tell Todd.

"Do you have any other surprising talents I should know about?" I asked him casually, masking the fact that I was dying to get his answer.

"A few, I guess. I play guitar, but I don't take it seriously."

"Cool! Have you ever played in a band? I can totally imagine you rocking out on stage." I needed to chill. I was being a little pushy.

"For a little while in high school. We argued all the

time, so I gave it up."

I dialed it back a bit, tried not to sound overly interested. "Anything else?"

"I can do a wall flip," Gray remarked casually.

"A what?" How does a wall flip work?

"A wall flip. Where you run up the wall then flip down to the ground."

"Oh, you cannot. That's stuff they do on TV," I said with a teasing grin.

"Only on TV, huh? I'll show you one day. I love to show off my talents." He laughed as he dished the gravy into a bowl. "With my luck, now I've bragged about it, I'll fall on my head."

I laughed along with him. "I hope you don't. I want to be impressed by both your cooking and your smooth moves." I put air quotes around "smooth moves," to let him know I still didn't believe he could do it.

A knock interrupted our mild flirtations. I started to get up and answer it.

"Freeze, lady," said Gray. "I'll get it." I grinned wryly and sat down.

He jogged over to the door, and I noticed he wore plaid sleep pants and a tight white tee. He filled out the pants perfectly.

According to my monitor, Arch and Wes stood in the hall. Gray let them in.

"It smells amazing in here!" Wes exclaimed. He sauntered over to me, also wearing sleep pants and a tee, black with the name of a band on it. He leaned forward and embraced me. "When you're feeling better, we'll reschedule our date." He kept his voice low as he released me. He didn't want his friends to overhear.

I stared blankly into his blue eyes, completely forgetting we scheduled a date.

"Remember, Ellie? Coffee?" He kept glancing at my head, concerned.

"Of course. I remember." I turned away and took a sip of juice to avoid blurting out the wrong thing. "I'd also like to reschedule for as soon as possible."

"Reschedule what?" Arch walked over to us and caught the tail end of our conversation. He still wore his neck brace and seemed uncomfortable.

Wes saved me from answering. "Coffee," he said casually. I averted my eyes. I didn't want to cause any jealousy or arguments. My various dates overwhelmed me: a theater date with Arch—hopefully to be rescheduled as well—a coffee date with Wes, and now a cooking date with Gray. The sensible voice in the back of my mind repeatedly asked me if any of them knew the others were interested. They knew Arch and I went on one—failed—date. Why else would we have been together, dressed up, when we crashed?

My stomach rumbled, causing Gray to stare at me from his position in the kitchen. "It's almost done, try not to starve to death."

I rolled my eyes at his sassiness. "I'll survive, thanks." I blew him a raspberry to drive my point home.

"If you do that again, I'll give your lips something to

do." Arch's voice behind me made my spine stiffen. The erotic tone to his voice shot straight to my, um, heart, and my insides became uncomfortably warm.

"I'll try to refrain," I whispered. Gray placed a plate full of food in front of me. *Saved by the gravy.* I decided to pretend calories cooked by gorgeous guys didn't count. I'd spend some time swimming soon to burn them off.

The plate in front of me overflowed with yumminess. I dug into my bacon, scrambled eggs, biscuits and gravy, hash browns, and grits. A traditional and delicious breakfast. "My mom used to cook breakfasts like this," I mumbled around a mouth full of egg. It took a moment for the guys to respond to my sudden over sharing.

"How old were you when she died?" asked Wes.

"I was eight, so some of the memories are vague. This is awesome." I smiled my thanks at Gray.

The guys made their own plates, and someone refilled my orange juice glass. I almost missed who it was because I tilted my head upward, moaning over the flavors invading my mouth with my first bite of gravy. I opened my eyes in time to watch Wes almost spill juice everywhere because he stared at me and not the juice pitcher in his hand. Gray's and Arch's attention was also on me. Arch scratched idly under his brace as he stared me down.

"What?" I asked.

"Nothing," said Wes. He stopped the flow of juice in time, and I slurped it down to keep it from spilling over the side.

"Why is everyone still staring at me?" I suspected their

minds were in the gutter, but feigned innocence.

Gray replied for the group. "I guess we're used to doing things together, no one else. It's kind of a novelty to have a lady in our mix."

"You don't date?" They were successful and hot. They'd have women banging down their doors.

"We do." Arch chimed in.

"We've all been searching for a more serious relationship, but in the meantime, we figured there's no harm in having fun," Wes tried to explain. "We haven't had an abundance of time the past few years, but when we do, we never introduce any of the girls to each other."

"Why not?" I asked.

"Don't get offended," said Arch. "But, girls are catty sometimes. We don't want to get any girls around each other to cause drama."

Gray continued where Arch left off. "We always planned on introducing any serious relationships to each other, but we haven't had many."

Another knock interrupted my musing about what it would take to be considered a serious relationship with any of these guys. They were picky.

I swiveled in my chair to see Todd and Rick on the monitor. Arch paused, waiting on my permission. "Do you want me to let them in?" he asked in a hushed tone.

"Yes, please. I'm surprised Todd didn't use his key." Time to face the music.

He opened the door, and Todd and Rick stopped inside the door. Todd's face morphed from worry to delight—I presumed because of the plethora of masculine sex appeal gathered in my apartment, all still wearing pajamas.

"*Hello*, pumpkin," Rick said. "We came to see what we could get you. We're making a grocery run."

Wes introduced himself to Rick first. "Hi, I'm Wes, a friend of Ellie's. I went to the grocery store last night, but I'd be happy to make any runs if she needs it. You don't have to go to any trouble."

I cocked my head at Wes, confused by the show. While his words were kind, I couldn't quite shake the comparison to a puffed-up rooster as I watched. Todd walked around him with an eye roll and hugged me tentatively. His arms barely touched me.

"It's okay, you can hug me. Don't bump my head is all." He squeezed tighter, and I awkwardly stood up to return the hug properly. "I'm still so sorry I worried you." I fought tears, guilt overwhelming me.

Rick put his arms around both of us and chastised me. "I thought he was going to come unglued. Never again, El. Never again."

I disentangled myself from their arms to look directly in their eyes when I apologized. "I really am sorry, guys. You're my family. I…" I trailed off. "I don't know what to say."

"We forgive you because we're best friends, and that's what we do. But, never again." Todd clapped his hands. "Now, what do you want from the store?" I gazed deep into Todd's eyes, blinked twice then widened my eyes.

There was no rhyme or reason to my eye movements except as a signal to him. I needed him to get something specific for me, something I didn't want the guys to know about.

He nodded once and tapped his nose to show he got the drift. Hopefully, he got the same drift I tried to send.

The rest of the list I verbalized. "Some gummy bears. And some cherry tomatoes. And that new book came out today." Todd, Rick, and I shared a love for cheesy vampire romance novels and the latest steamy one just came out. "I'd love to read it while I'm resting this weekend."

"You got it, pumpkin." Todd kissed my cheek before pulling Rick toward the hall. "See you shortly."

Three men swung their gazes to me as the door closed. "Why wouldn't you ask me for those things at the store?" Wes asked.

"I would've, but they were going anyway. And if you must know, I didn't want to tell you which book we're reading."

Arch burst out laughing. "Why in the world not?"

"People like you tend to make fun of books like it."

They began to shift in their seats, offended. Oops. I'd stuck my foot in my mouth. "People like us? What does that mean?" asked Arch.

I grew more embarrassed. "I don't know! Hip, cool... You know what I mean."

Gray gawked at me like I was a life-sized Rubik's cube. "You think we're hip and cool and that you aren't?" *Didn't I say that already?*

"Uh... Yeah. I'm a bookworm. A nerd." I shrugged my shoulders. I didn't mind being different from them. I'd never had a problem with being dorky. "It doesn't mean I don't enjoy your company, and I assume you enjoy mine. I'm guessing you like being my friends or you wouldn't be here."

Significant glances passed among the three of them. Arch spoke first. "You're right about that. If we didn't like being around you, we wouldn't be here. But we don't look at ourselves any differently." He snorted. "You think we can't be nerdy? Gray has an enormous comic book collection; Wes had acne until he was twenty, and me? I write Star Wars fan fiction."

The room went silent. If my expression matched Gray's and Wes's, I had wide eyes, eyebrows nearly to my hairline, and a gaping mouth. Gray recovered first.

"*Dude.* You write Star Wars fan fiction? I don't even know how to feel about that."

"Like, what kind of fan fiction?" I asked.

"Please say smutty Leia," Wes begged.

Poor Arch looked like he regretted his confession. I tried to spare him by fighting the laughter back. "It's no big deal. Something I do after work sometimes, to wind down. I've got quite a large following online. It's no worse than owning eight hundred comic books!" He glared at Gray accusingly.

"It is *so much* worse than owning eight hundred comic books!" Gray's voice sounded like a thirteen-year-old going through puberty as he tried to talk through his laughter.

My giggles erupted from my chest; I couldn't hold them in anymore. "Okay," I said through my chuckles. "Arch and Gray, you're dorky enough to hang out with me, but Wes, having acne isn't enough. I need something else."

"There is nothing else. I'm cool. Always have been." He wouldn't meet my eyes.

Arch snorted. "Try again, homie."

Wes flashed me an innocent smile that didn't fool me for a second. "I swear, Ellie, I've never done anything embarrassing."

"I've got two words for you, man," said Gray. "Peter Pan."

Wes's face blanched. "Gray Baron Morales! You promised!" Wes brought out the big guns, using Gray's whole name.

Arch nearly bounced up and down with uncontained exuberance. "Why don't I know about Peter Pan? What's Peter Pan mean?" The neck brace made his excitement more comical. He turned his entire upper body to look from one of us to another.

We all stared at Gray, waiting on him to spill Wes's secrets. He grinned, furrowing his eyebrows evilly. "Sorry, *Wesley*. She needs to know you're normal, too." He rocked a little before the words flew from his mouth. "Guys, Wes played Peter Pan in a community theater production in high school. He wore tights and everything."

I couldn't picture the enormous blond man wearing

tights, prancing around on a stage as Peter Pan. It was easier to imagine him on a football field or playing volleyball on a beach.

"That's not embarrassing, Wes," I said in an attempt to console his bruised ego. "I think the ability to act is an admirable quality."

"I didn't mention the best part, then," said Gray cheerfully. "He was horrible. He forgot all his lines. Tripped like three times. Stepped on the fairy's toes. It was ridiculous. I don't even know how he *got* the part."

"Okay. That part's pretty funny," I said, and my giggles renewed. Wes even started to chuckle.

"I guess it *was* pretty silly. I'd always wanted to be in a play, and I tried it. I hated it. I hated memorizing lines and getting all dressed up." He shrugged. "I never did it again." He paused for a moment, considering. "Except when I became a lawyer. We act all the time. But that's totally different. There are no tights," he deadpanned before leaning back in his chair, face pensive once again. "But, if it helps you realize we aren't as cool as you think we are, I do love to read. I love to read all sorts of stuff. Vampires, werewolves, classics, spy books, comedies, you name it." We all forgot about finishing our meal, too wrapped up in the confessions of our dorky sides.

The remains of breakfast hardened on our plates as we talked. Todd stopped by and passed me a small box hidden in a brown paper bag. I peeked inside and found a box of tampons. I snickered. "I knew you'd know what I meant." He blew me a kiss and left to spend the day with his love.

When he left, Gray and Wes commanded Arch and I go take naps while they cleaned up the kitchen.

I insisted everyone go home when they finished with the kitchen chores. I wouldn't take my nap until they agreed. While I appreciated their kindness and care, it was time for me to return to my regular life.

CHAPTER SEVEN

Two days later, a tap sounded at my door in the middle of rereading my smutty vampire romance novel. To answer it, I disentangled Satan from my lap. Wes stood in the hall holding a tablet in his hand, wearing another band t-shirt and jeans that looked sewn on. "Hey, Wes! Come in." I belatedly realized I'd left the monitor off again.

"I wanted to drop this off," he said as he came into the living room. "I hoped you wouldn't be in class."

"I took the day off. I'm still pretty sore." I pointed to the object in his hands. "A tablet?"

"Yeah, it's got all my books on it." He handed it to me.

"Why would you bring me all your books?" I sat on the couch and tapped the home button. Wes sat beside me and reached over to touch a reading app that brought up his library. I watched him as he fiddled with the app. He tucked his hair behind his ear, but it kept falling out and brushing his cheekbone, not long enough to stay. I resisted the urge to neaten the rogue lock of hair.

"I wanted to show you I'm like you. We aren't that different. I only appear like I belong on a surfboard. In reality, I belong with my nose in a book." My mind strayed to images of him reading a book on the beach. *Stop that! You're so dirty lately! Think about the gift!*

My voice left me. "I don't know what to say. This is touching."

"Don't get excited. I want it back in a few weeks—enough time for you to learn what I like and write down some titles you'd like to have. Everything I own is on there, even copies of my hardcover books. No matter where I am or what device I have with me, I can pull up any book I've read and read it again." I needed to do the same with my own library.

"That's a good idea. I still prefer an actual book in hand, but the world is going digital. Plus, if there was a fire, at least I'd still have my entire library at my fingertips." I smiled up at his pleased expression. Me perusing his library excited him. "So, how was your day?"

"Great, actually. We're starting a nasty case where the defendant has been framed. That's all I can tell you, though. We're working on proof that it was a frame-up."

"We can't talk about my case either, can we?" There wasn't much to talk about. I could only wait for my lawyers to get all their depositions and ducks in a row.

"Not if we want to continue to be—friends. Ellie, I

see myself definitely wanting more than friendship. I wanted to throw that out there." Not knowing how to respond, I leaned my head against the couch to contemplate the information and ended up resting my head on Wes's arm. His hard, warm, muscular arm. He placed it on the back of the couch without my realizing it. I jumped forward. "I'm sorry!"

He chuckled sexily rather than comically. "It's okay, Ellie. You're always welcome to lay your head on me." My blush answered his question. "Okay. I've embarrassed you enough for one day. I'll go. I'm meeting the guys for dinner to discuss a case and the depositions we took today. I'll text you later?"

"That sounds good. Todd should be here soon. We will plan our coffee date soon?" I enjoyed myself every time I was with him. I wanted more time with him.

"I'd love it." He got up from the couch, and I made a move to follow. "No, don't get up. I know the way out." I nodded my head, and he let himself out. I squealed once I knew he couldn't hear me. How romantic! He brought me every book he'd read to help me get to know him better. It was personal and a bold move.

Before I started combing through the book list, I called Todd.

"Todd, please tell me you have five minutes to act like a teenage girl with me." He always enjoyed wigging out with me.

"I always have time to act like a teenage girl with you, pumpkin. You know that."

"Perfect. Guess what Wes brought me?" He'd never guess such an unusual gift. The gift showed Wes put a lot of consideration into what I appreciated.

"A kitten?"

"No." *Dork.*

"A sub sandwich and a pint of vodka?"

"No, and what the hell?" He was weird sometimes.

"It's what I'd like to have right now."

I threw myself onto the couch, phone clasped to my ear. "No! He brought me a tablet!"

He gasped. "It's full of dirty movies isn't it?"

"No! What's wrong with you? I mean… I guess it *could* be. I haven't checked. But, no! It's full of every book he's ever read." How did he remember every book he'd ever read? I certainly couldn't remember each book I'd read since childhood.

"How many books is that?"

"I only glanced at the list, but it's incredibly long."

"Why would he bring you that?"

"Because he wants me to get to know him better, and since I love to read, he thought this would be a great way." He was right.

"Well, that's the most romantic thing I've ever heard. Jesus, these guys are too damn good to be true."

"Todd, how am I going to pick one of them? They've all three made it clear they're interested." I prayed they weren't too good to be true.

"Cross that bridge when you come to it. Get to know them. You'll lean more toward one of them as you learn more about them.

"You're right. I know you're right. You're always right." He was right a frustrating amount of the time.

"Damn skippy. Now go pore over his books and learn more about this hunky lawyer." He disconnected without letting me say goodbye. Typical Todd.

The tablet was chock full of books. Long books, short books. From wholesome, family friendly books to books you could never let your grandma know you read. From classics to… well, not classics. He even had an entire section devoted to digital comics. I could get lost in his tablet for weeks.

His variety impressed me. It said a lot about him as a person. He had to be open-minded, and his career was probably easier to come by for him than for others. After spending the evening browsing, I fell asleep with his tablet on my chest and a smile on my face.

The next morning, I opened my front door to grab my newspaper and came face to face with Arch. He stood outside his apartment with a ravishingly beautiful woman. He wore a robe and slippers, but she was dressed like she was prepared to go to an exclusive night club. Standing next to her in my owl pajama pants and *I Read for Pleasure* t-shirt made me feel inadequate. But then, half the supermodels in the world would feel inadequate next to this woman.

I pulled myself together enough to speak. "Good morning." I scooped my paper up and scurried into my apartment, switching on my security monitor.

If anyone watched me after I closed the door, they would've committed me. My hair was in a messy bun, mascara smeared under my eyes, and my hands pressed against the wall on either side of the monitor. I leaned in to try to take in every moment of their exchange.

The woman kept trying to put her arms around Arch and cuddle up to him. He was clearly uncomfortable, and his gaze repeatedly drifted to my apartment door. She was an octopus—every time he'd remove her hand she'd find a way to touch him again. Finally, a muffled yelling came through my door. The monitor showed Arch jerking away from the woman, face angry and red. I assumed he'd taken all he could and snapped.

Ms. Hot, Sexy, and Slutty eventually turned and stomped down the hall toward the elevators. As soon as she walked out of my camera's view, Arch jumped to my door and banged his fist on it.

He moved so fast it startled me. I leaped away from the monitor as if he could see me spying on him. The sharp knocks on the wood reverberated in my gut. Before I answered, I took a few deep breaths to compose myself. I didn't want him to know I spied on him. As he walked in, I realized the monitor was still on. I hit the power button with my elbow as he rushed into the room.

"Ellie, I'm so sorry."

"What do you have to be sorry about?" I feigned innocence, as if the beautiful woman didn't make me feel like a fool for thinking Arch liked me. He seemed angry with her, giving me hope I misunderstood the exchange, and he hadn't spent the night with her.

"That woman. Monica." He stepped toward me, arms out, apologetic.

"What about her? I don't understand what's going on." I turned to the kitchen before my lies showed on my face. "Would you like some tea?"

"No, thank you. Listen. Monica didn't spend the night. She showed up this morning, I guess hoping to catch me. I've managed to avoid her for weeks. We had a few dates a couple of months ago. She wasn't for me, so I broke it off. She stopped by or called every few weeks since then." He followed me into the kitchen.

"Arch, you don't have to explain yourself to me." Inside, I begged him to keep explaining himself to me.

"I want to. I do. I've been trying to be nice to her up until now. But when you saw that, I was afraid you'd think she had spent the night."

"Why?" Why would he care about my opinion? I yearned for him to care, given how I'd begun to care for him, but if he did, I needed him to spell it out for me.

"Why what?" He blinked, bewildered. He didn't understand how I could be confused by his actions.

"Why were you worried about my reaction to Monica?" When it came down to it, what right did I have to be upset if she spent the night?

Arch recoiled with a face like I'd slapped him. "I... I don't know. I thought... I thought we had something. A connection. Was I wrong?"

"No," I murmured. "You weren't wrong. I felt a

connection." My inner self did cartwheels. He wanted a deeper relationship with me.

"Then, you understand why I got upset?"

I sighed in resignation. "Of course, I do." I decided to go for honesty. "I got upset, too. Then, I felt stupid because we aren't a couple, and we've no ties to each other." I threw my hands up in consternation. "We've been on one failed attempt at a date, and that's it. I've been flirting with you, but I've also been flirting with your partners!" *Why did I say that out loud?* "So, I felt stupid assuming you weren't dating anyone." The cat definitely escaped the bag. I admitted I liked all of them.

"So, you've been flirting with them." He turned away, then back to me, his entire body tense.

"Well... yeah." The *World's Biggest Ass* award was being engraved with my name as we spoke.

"It's okay." His expression said it was *not* okay.

"What do you want me to say? All three of you flirted with me, showed interest in me, and asked me out." I began to panic, afraid to lose their friendship and potential relationships before they even happened. "You don't know me, yet, but I don't go on dates every weekend. I don't play the field. I'm waiting for someone I have a real connection with." I screwed up my nerve to continue. "I've felt a connection with all three of you."

"It's okay! You're right. You should get to know us before making any decisions." He looked determined, like he would ensure I chose him. "So, I'm going to go get ready for work. And I'm going to pretend none of this happened."

I nodded my head as he walked away, baffled by the events of the morning. I couldn't find any words to say, so I gaped at him. He turned around and lifted his chin, which I returned, slack-jawed.

Still dumbfounded, I made my way to the bathroom to take a shower and get ready for my day. I winced when I saw myself in the mirror—I was a mess. My hair was a total rat's nest, and a huge zit popped up on my chin.

With an important class first thing, I didn't have time to mourn my disheveled state. I slapped on the minimal makeup Todd painstakingly taught me to apply without taking a lot of time or effort. I wasted no time on my hair, a quick wash and blow dry. I ended up looking nice, though not a knockout. I'd take it.

My morning was uneventful until I walked out of my class. Gray stood outside the classroom with two coffees in hand. He wore another tight-fitting polo and slacks, his dark hair up in a bun. "Hello there," I said, surprised to find him suddenly on campus.

"Pardon the intrusion, but I checked, and you don't have another class today." He handed me a cup. "A certain best friend of yours might've given me his number after the wreck, you know, just in case, and I might've called him to find out how you take your coffee and what your day looks like today." He handed me one of the cups. "Please don't think I'm creepy. I had reason to be here."

The coffee tasted like rich hazelnut. "You even got the right creamer. Brownie points to Gray. The hazelnut cancels the creepiness a bit. Did you have a lecture?"

He handed me a paper bag I hadn't noticed. "No brownies, but I did get cinnamon breakfast cake. Todd *might've* mentioned that, too." He grinned, pleased, teeth sparkling in the morning sunshine. "Yes, I just finished it. It was a speech of sorts, not a whole class."

I peered down into the bag. "He's a gem, and so are you." Cinnamon cake was my weakness, and I hadn't taken the time to eat before class.

After my morning with Arch, having Gray drop by for a visit made me wonder what I'd done to warrant such attention.

His smile was hot enough to melt my heart, full of boyish charm with a hint of the strong man behind it. When one of his eyebrows rose, I shook myself out of my scrutiny. "There's a nice seating area a few minutes' walk from here. Would you like to go sit down?" I asked.

"Sure. Lead the way."

We strolled along, sipping coffee. "Tell me about your family," I asked as we reached the benches. We sat under a sprawling magnolia and enjoyed the warm autumn day.

"I have a big family. They live in Atlanta, near Arch and Wes's families. Nine brothers and sisters."

"*Nine?* My goodness. Your parents must be exhausted. Where are you in the pecking order?" I imagined how loud his home must've been.

"I'm oldest. Yeah, my parental units…" He took a breath before continuing. "They're a little odd, but loveable. My youngest brother is four. They swear they're done having kids, but I wouldn't be surprised if another one is born."

"That's kind of awesome. They must really love each other and the kids." A huge family held no real appeal to me. Kudos to those who wanted it, but no chance I'd push ten children out of my nether region.

"There was a *lot* of love in my house, for sure. My parents didn't want me to go into law. But for as long as I can remember that's all Arch, Wes, and I talked about. It's all we've ever wanted to do."

"Y'all grew up together?" They certainly acted like brothers.

"Yeah, our parents were close friends. Tight knit. They still are, as a matter of fact."

"Arch made it seem like he wasn't close to his parents, though." Curiosity ate me up inside.

"Yeah, he's not. None of us are, really. Not anymore."

"Why?" I tried not to sound too eager for the answer. I sipped my coffee and stared out over the large, grand landscape. A century old, the age of the campus pressed against me. If I could listen well enough, I would be able to hear the stories it had to tell.

"Like I said, they didn't want me to be a lawyer. None of our parents did. They wanted us to go into the family business."

"Family business?" Like the mafia?

"Farming. They own a large, successful farm on the outskirts of Atlanta. It's become quite lucrative, and they wanted us to take over the farm when they got old enough to retire. The three families share the responsibilities and the success of the farm."

"Wow! I'd no idea you three were farmhands! You look like you were born in a courtroom; you're so comfortable in your suits." Their suits were incredibly sexy, but I wouldn't mind seeing them in work clothes.

Gray let out a booming laugh. "We *hate* wearing suits. All three of us. That's the one part of being lawyers we'll all agree sucks. We're more comfortable wearing jeans and flannels." He sipped his coffee. "I take it back. Arch loves it, even though he denies it."

I chuckled. "What does your family farm?"

"They have a section like a petting zoo, small garden, and so on. They do tours of the farm, host classrooms, have birthday parties, that sort of thing. And in the fall, they do pumpkin patches, hayrides, and a corn maze. It brings in some great revenue, but the real money is in the cotton. They have contracts with some huge clothiers and provide them with raw cotton."

"Impressive. I bet they have a lot of employees." It sounded like a ton of work.

He paused for a moment, considering his words carefully. "Not as many as you might assume, but their numbers are growing. It was pretty contained to family when we were growing up, but one of Wes's sisters took a liking to the retail side of it. Now there is also a branch making soap from our goats' milk and other artisan skin care using ingredients off the farm. She sells it online and is building it up quite nicely." He finished his coffee and set it on the bench beside me. He reached over me to do it and got close enough I could smell his skin. He smelled like leather and a little bit like... bacon? I suppressed a shiver. It was both sexy and made me a little hungry.

As he leaned back to his own side of the bench, his shirt shifted, and I spied the tip of a tattoo on his neck. How had I never noticed it before? I'd have to get the whole picture to decide if I found it attractive or not. Normally, I wasn't a big fan of tattoos, but his intrigued me. *Just reach over and pull his shirt down and look at it.* I shook my head at myself, luckily while Gray looked away.

"Tell me more about you, Ellie."

"You know a lot already." Talking about myself made my skin crawl.

"I know about your parents, and you like to read. Tell me something about *you*."

"I like to sing." I wasn't necessarily *good* at it, but I liked it.

"Oh? Sing something for me."

"No!" I laughed. "You're crazy. I used to sing in school, all through middle and high school. I had quite a few solos," I said with pride. "My mom sang, too. It helped me stay close to her after she... left me." Too bad if you didn't use it you lost it. I couldn't sing a lick anymore.

"One day, Ellie Asche, I'll hear those pipes."

I rubbed his arm consolingly and a little flirtatiously. "Sure, dear. Whatever you say."

The last few sips of coffee were cold and

unappetizing. I twisted my lips into a wry smile. "I guess it's about time for our coffee date to be over. I promised Todd I'd meet him after class to go grocery shopping. Both of our pantries are bare."

"Alas, dear lady. The grocery cart calls thee."

I giggled at his ridiculous accent. "We should do this again sometime. I'd like to learn more about growing up on a farm."

"And I'll think of ways to get you to sing for me." He winked.

"You can try." I snorted. "Thank you for the coffee."

He reached over and lifted my hand, giving it the lightest brushing of a kiss. The intimate gesture caused my chest to rise and fall rapidly. I controlled my breathing. He didn't need to know how he affected me. "You're welcome, sweet lady. Can I offer you a ride to the grocery store?"

"No, thank you," I said, shy after his kiss. "I brought my car today."

"Then, goodbye. I'll text you about another date."

"Sounds wonderful." My face held a goofy smile. With dreamy eyes, I watched him walk away. My gaze lingered on his backside and the way it curved in his well-tailored suit for a moment longer than propriety called for, then I turned and practically skipped to my car. I couldn't wait to fill Todd in. It'd been an exciting day, and it wasn't even noon yet.

CHAPTER EIGHT

"*Then,* he kissed my hand and said he'd text me to make another date!" Todd and I rounded out our grocery trip in the produce department, loading up on fresh fruits and veggies.

"How do you get yourself into these sorts of situations?" he asked as he thumped on a watermelon. His voice sounded jealous. "I mean, up until my whirlwind courtship with Rick, my love life has always been bor-ring. Thank God for that man."

"How has mine been eventful? This is the first time anything like this has ever happened to me!" I grabbed a bag to hold several cucumbers. "I've never mixed into a love triangle… hell, this isn't even a love triangle! It's a love square!"

"Darlin', this love thing you've got going on is more interesting than anything else we have in our lives right now, so enjoy the ride while it lasts." He placed a bag of onions in the cart.

"Secretly, I'm hoping to hear from Wes tonight."

"Grab the bull by the horns and call him yourself!"

I stopped short, hand halfway to the apples. "I couldn't do that!"

"Why the hell not?" Todd added a few more apples to my bag before tying it off.

"I don't know! I never have."

"Now's a great time to start. Text him when you get home and tell him to be over at six for dinner. You're cooking for him. Then, the ball will be in his court." He spoke with his hands, waving them around. "Make your lasagna. It's to die for."

"But it's such a simple meal. Shouldn't I make something more complicated?" Would my lasagna impress him enough to make him think I could cook everything as well as I could cook lasagna?

Todd turned to the checkout. "It is simple, but it's delicious. And make your homemade cheesy garlic bread to go with it. I'll be expecting leftovers for dinner tomorrow night, please and thank you."

My metaphorical backbone straightened itself, and I turned the cart toward the dairy. "Let's go get some cheese then. I didn't get enough to make lasagna."

"Now you're talking. Do you have enough garlic?"

"Please." I rolled my eyes. "I always have enough garlic."

Once I found all the ingredients I could possibly need,

we checked out and headed home. I started the lasagna the minute I got home, knowing it would taste better if I put it in the fridge to set for a few hours before reheating it for dinner.

Todd turned up soon after I got there. He must've put his groceries up and headed over right away.

"Did you text him yet?"

"Not yet, I wanted to get this started. It would've been tastier if I'd made it last night." A few hours in the fridge should do the trick.

"What if he has plans and you're making a huge, delicious lasagna for no reason?"

I paused my unpacking. "You're saying the lasagna will go to waste if he doesn't come over?" That'd be the day.

"Heck, no! Text him, already! You're stalling."

"Fine!" I grabbed my phone off the counter.

Ellie: Hey! Do you have plans for dinner tonight?

"There. Sent. Are you happy?" I scowled at Todd.

"Yes. But I'll be happier when you get his reply." Luckily for Todd's nerves, it came through quickly.

Wes: I'm free after six. Would you like to go out to eat?

I studied at my watch. I had plenty of time.

Ellie: Come to my apartment. I've already started dinner. Bring a big appetite.

Ellie: Wait, do you have any allergies?

Wes: Just Penicillin. Try not to put any antibiotics in the food, and we'll be fine.

I laughed and breathed a sigh of relief at the same

time.

Ellie: Deal. See you at six thirty.

Todd read the texts over my shoulder. "Why do you spell everything out? You've always done that. There are text shortcuts, you know."

"I hate them. There's no reason we can't be grammatically correct whenever possible." I lectured. "Forget those kids and their texting fads. And they can get off my lawn while they're at it." I giggled at myself.

Todd rolled his eyes. "Whatever. I'm going to go pick out your dinner outfit. He'll be wearing a suit from work. You don't want to look like a slob next to him." He waltzed toward my bedroom, humming. He enjoyed my flirtations far more than I did. He didn't have to worry about the hard part when multiple relationships got more serious. He only focused on the fun.

The lasagna came together beautifully. I'd made it so many times it was second nature. Once it was in the oven, I wandered into my room to find Todd in my closet, reorganizing again.

"Isn't it time to donate some stuff? I'm never going to wear the skinny jeans. Ever." There are some dresses in there not appropriate to wear in the bedroom, much less out of the house.

"Puhlease. You're smashing in anything I pick out for you. But, I thought along the same lines. There are some styles in here at least a couple of years old. It's been ages since we organized. I love organizing your clothes." Todd came out of the neatened closet with straight-legged gray slacks and a blue silk button up shirt covered with white polka dots. It had cap sleeves and a ruffle at the neck. Satan followed him out. He loved Todd.

"Todd, I'm impressed. I love the outfit." It was cute and feminine, but I wouldn't feel like a peacock in it.

He grinned a Cheshire cat grin at me. "Good, then you'll let me play with your hair and add another layer of mascara."

I ignored him. "When does Rick get off work?" I asked.

"He's been working a ton of hours, still the work audit. It'll be late."

I rolled my eyes and plopped down on the bed. "Aw, I'm sorry. But it won't last long, and you'll get your lovey back."

With several hours before Wes was due to arrive, we opted to pile up in bed and watch Netflix.

All too soon, the lasagna was ready to chill. The wine breathed in the bucket. The bread was about to go in the oven. Todd perched behind me on the bed, leisurely putting curls into my hair as we laughed at the show.

The doorbell interrupted our makeup session a few minutes later. "I'll get it," I said.

I remembered to check the monitor. Arch stood in the hall. I opened the door to find him visibly irritated. "Don't you know how to answer your phone?" he asked as he pushed past me into the apartment. "Are you okay?"

"Hello, Arch. It's nice to see you." My sarcasm game was on point as he barged in. "Would you like to come in?

Oh, good. You'd like to."

"We've been worried!" he replied as he yanked his phone out of his pocket. "I've got to text the guys and let them know you're fine." His fingers flew across his phone as he presumably notified his friends of my safety status.

"My phone hasn't made a peep!" I marched into the bedroom to find Todd trying to perch himself on the bed to peer out of the bedroom. He jerked back as soon as I stormed in. "Hand me my phone, Todd, *please.*"

He complied. I tapped the home button to find three missed calls and seven missed texts. All three of them had tried repeatedly to get a hold of me. I pulled down the settings menu to find the phone silenced.

"It's on silent. I didn't hear any of this, did you?" Todd shook his head. I turned to find Arch approaching my bedroom. "Honestly, don't you think you're overreacting a little?" I asked Arch.

Arch stood in my doorway, speechless. The fading bruises around his eyes were prominent, and his mouth slack-jawed. "Overreacting?" he spat out. "Anything could've happened to you. Wes hears from you one moment, then the next you drop off the face of the earth. We thought you were dead."

It was my turn to be speechless and gawk at him. "What if I was asleep? Or, you know, my phone was on silent? It seems like you borrowed a little trouble today. Besides, who says it's your job to worry about me?" I was incensed. "First of all, I'm not anyone's to worry about, yet. Maybe someday, but not at this point. I won't be smothered, not for one moment."

"But—"

"Second of all, next time, call Todd. Or, I have a landline here. You could've called that number. It's in all the paperwork I filled out at your office. You didn't think about that, did you?" He freaked out, over nothing.

Arch gazed back and forth between Todd and me. Then, his face shut down, and he whirled around and marched out of the apartment, slamming the front door behind him. Todd scrambled off the bed and joined me in time to watch him storm out.

"Daaamn. Boy is *pissed*." Todd tugged me to the bed. "Let's get you finished."

That surprised me. "Shouldn't I go after him?"

"Nope. We don't know why in the world he's overreacting. You'll argue. When he calms down, he'll realize he overreacted, and he'll come talk to you. Let it ride."

"I guess." I worried I ran him off for good with my talk of smothering, but I figured Todd had more experience with upset men than I did. The TV show lost its appeal, so I brooded while he finished my makeup. I ended up looking fantastic, but as though I hadn't put in any effort. He really was a genius.

We packed up the mess we'd made all afternoon, and Todd left with a huge chunk of chilled lasagna. With only about thirty minutes left until Wes arrived, I put the lasagna in the oven on a low temp to warm. I then proceeded to pace my apartment until the knock from Wes came.

My nerves were shot. I'd already spent a significant amount of time with these guys. I had no reason to be apprehensive. But my altercation with Arch wasn't sitting right with me. Something was majorly off about the whole encounter.

Wes knocked a second time before I came out of my contemplations. When the second rap sounded, I scurried over to open it. "I'm sorry, Wes! Please, come in."

"No problem! It smells delicious in here."

"Thank you. We're eating simple tonight, but I think you'll like it." He'd better like it. I didn't know how to make anything better.

"I'm sure I will if you made it. What're we having?"

"Lasagna with garlic bread and Italian wine. And if you'd like, a salad while the lasagna finishes up."

"I'd love a salad. One question though. Do you put fruit in your salads?"

What a ridiculous question. "Fruit goes into fruit salad. Vegetables go into salad. I don't mix the two."

"Marry me." The twinkle in his gray-blue eyes told me he joked, but a rock still dropped into my gut. The imaginary rock vibrated and sent tingles all over me.

"Maybe after I see how well you cook."

"Deal." He followed me into the kitchen and helped me put a salad together. We were compatible in the salad-prep department. We agreed on every ingredient except celery.

"I'm sorry, Ellie. Your taste in salads is ruined by the

celery. It's an abomination." He laughed at his little joke and turned toward the fridge to grab the salad dressing to put on top of his carefully prepared stack of veggies. While his back was turned, I dumped the entire pile of celery I'd chopped for my salad into his bowl.

"What the heck?" He glared at me, eyes narrow.

I tried to stay straight faced, but couldn't stop the laughter. Wes picked the celery out one by one and threw it at me. Little did he know, over the years, Todd and I practiced the art of catching food in our mouths until we mastered it. Celery was no challenge. After I caught three in a row he became more impressed.

"That's quite the hidden talent you have there!"

"Thank you kindly, sir." I curtsied.

He threw another piece of celery and kept going until I missed on number eight. We stopped then and took our salads to the table. After we sat, Wes studied me for a minute, contemplating his words. When he spoke, he acknowledged the elephant in the room we'd worked to ignore.

"Ellie, I need to tell you something about Arch. Something he probably won't be able to tell you himself, at least not for a while. I shouldn't be telling you now, but you need to know."

"Okay." I imagined all sorts of scenarios, the least scary was Arch thought I was a troll but wanted my money for his firm.

"If he cares about someone, he can't stand not being able to get a hold of them." My eyebrows furrowed with indignation. Wes stopped picking at his salad. "It's not like he needs to know where you are at all moments of the day. He's not controlling or anything. But if he randomly needs to get a hold of you and doesn't hear back quickly, he gets major anxiety."

"Why?" I couldn't understand why he'd freak out over something so minute.

"See, that's the private part. Arch has only been in one serious relationship in his life." Wes sighed. "Enough time has passed; I hope he doesn't get mad at me for this."

"One?" I asked in disbelief.

"He's had dates, sure, but Penny was different. She went to school with us, we grew up around her. She knew our parents, knew the farm—Gray said he told you about the farm?"

"Yeah, it sounds kinda idyllic."

He took a big bite of salad before replying. "It kind of was, kind of wasn't. That's a whole 'nother story though."

"Okay, so she was his high school sweetheart?"

"Right. We were in school at Emory. It was great because of how close to home it was. We were all there, the three of us and Penny."

"How old were you?"

"Juniors. Arch and Penny had an apartment off campus. Gray and I had one beside it, same floor and everything." He paused to clear his throat. "They were pretty serious. He bought a ring, but she didn't know it yet. They talked about all aspects of their future. It was all planned out. They even discussed kids."

He stopped to clear his throat again. I jumped up. "Let me get you some wine." I scurried into the kitchen and soon returned with a glass.

"Thanks, I had some lettuce stuck." He took a few big gulps. "One day, Arch texted Penny to call him after her morning class. He had some question to ask her. Something about dinner or some such. She never called. He wasn't worried, assumed she missed his text or got busy or something." He gulped down some more wine. "He waited until he knew she was done with her afternoon class and called. She didn't answer. He kept calling all evening. When it got so late she couldn't possibly still be held up at class, he called us, and we started searching for her."

"Why didn't he call the police? Or her parents?" My salad wilted in front of me, forgotten. I sipped my wine mindlessly as I listened to the tragic story, tears gathering in my eyes. I foresaw a tragic ending.

"He did. The police basically blew him off, of course. Her parents freaked and joined us in the search. From what he could tell, she could've disappeared before she even got to her first class. We hacked into her e-mail, found one from her study group, and contacted them. They confirmed she never made her morning class."

"My god, what happened to her?" My heart hurt, knowing where he was going with the story.

"We couldn't search well in the dark, though we tried. It wasn't until daylight that we found her car." He shook his head, the pain of the memories on his face. "It happened in the winter. Atlanta winters are mild, but the temperature had dropped pretty low the night before. The best we could tell, she hit a patch of black ice and went off the road." He took another moment to drain his glass.

I filled it up. At this rate, he'd be drunk before the lasagna. If it was that hard for *him* to share the story, I couldn't imagine how hard it must be for Arch to tell it. Wes sighed. "Her brown sedan blended in with the branches and trees in the ditch, and no one spotted it. By the time we found her, she was dead. She would've made it if the wreck had been found sooner, but she had a bleed on her brain. That's what killed her."

My heart thumped painfully. "I don't even know what to say." I had to find Arch. I had to tell him I understood, and I'd be considerate of his feelings. "Wes, I'm so sorry to do this to you, but I have to go apologize to Arch. Would you be upset if I invited him to join us?"

Wes leaned in and kissed my cheek, a move that shocked and pleased me. "I'm glad you want to. It's been years, and I think he's ready for another commitment, but it'll be a pain he never escapes."

I jumped up, ran across the hall to Arch's apartment, and rapped my knuckles on his door. No answer. "Arch," I called. "Open up!" With still no answer, I knocked harder, closed-fist. "Come on, Arch! I need to talk to you."

Just as I gave up and turned to my apartment, dejected, he answered. I whirled around to Arch glaring at me from his entry. He left the door open as he turned back into his apartment. I took it as my cue to enter.

The catchy theme song from a classic video game filled the air as Arch grabbed his controller, jumping on turtles and shooting fire at moving plants, as he staunchly refused to look at me.

"Hey." Once I was inside, I had no idea how to bring up the subject.

He rolled his eyes at my attempt to make conversation while ignoring the greater issue at hand.

I scrambled for something to say. I didn't know how to bring up Penny. I pointed to his paintings, abstract and alluring. "Your artwork is intriguing. Is it by anyone I'd know?"

"The artist only goes by Coleman. He's unknown, but I love him. I buy everything of his I can find."

"Oh." I couldn't come up with anything else to put off what I needed to say, so I blurted out, "I didn't come over here to talk about your decorations."

"You don't say?" he said in mock surprise. He paused his game and turned on the couch to face me. "What do you want, Ellie?"

"I want to apologize. Wes told me about Penny."

The color drained out of Arch's face. "He shouldn't have."

"Maybe not. But, I understand why you got upset. And I'm sorry I came down hard on you. Knowing what you've been through, I don't blame you at all for panicking." I wanted to hug and comfort him.

"I didn't panic." His gaze shifted to his couch, and he began to pick absently at a string.

"You were pretty anxious by the time you got to my apartment." *To say the least.*

"I was worried. Don't I have a right to be concerned for a friend? Would you have gotten mad if it had been Todd upset?"

"Todd and I have been friends—family—for a whole lotta years. He's *earned* the right to know where I am at any given moment." I sat down on the couch beside him. "And, Arch, I'm not saying we won't get to that point. We might, whether it's as friends or something more." I touched his hand so he'd look at me. "But, right now, we aren't there. However, now I know what you've been through, I can definitely make allowances. I'll be more aware of my phone and check it more often."

"I'll never not love her." He caught my gaze and held it. His expression and tone of voice was defiant. He expected me to argue.

"I'd never expect you to stop, no matter what happens between the two of us. Any woman worth building a relationship with would never ask you to stop caring for Penny." I took his hand. "I like you, Arch. I'm pretty sure you like me. I won't ask you to talk about Penny. You don't ever have to, but if you'd like to, I'm here to listen. Again, I'm sorry I got upset earlier. I didn't know."

"I've never talked about her to anyone but people who knew her. No other woman in my life has ever even heard her name." He squeezed my hand as he pondered the situation. "I guess I'm glad you know. I don't know if I'll want to talk, but I'm relieved it's not something I have to go through recounting it myself. One day I'll tell you, in my own words."

I smiled; glad he made peace with me knowing. "I made dinner for Wes and me. Would you please come join us?"

"I don't want to intrude."

"I already talked to him about it, and it would be no intrusion. Please, come over."

"What're we having?" He narrowed his eyes, my answer the deciding factor if he'd eat at home or at my place.

"Salad, lasagna, and garlic bread."

His eyes lit up. He jumped up and pulled me by our still-joined hands toward the food at my place. "I love lasagna. It's my favorite."

CHAPTER NINE

Dinner was a hit. They loved the lasagna enough to call Gray over to eat with us. His first bite, accompanied with a long moan, made me feel like a million bucks.

Wes finished last and ate more than anyone else. Even Gray beat him after getting a late start. When he ate his last bite, he leaned back as far as his chair would allow and sighed. "Ellie, if you keep cooking for us, we'll all have to spend more time in the gym."

"Hey! Not true. I don't cook like this all the time. Since you three came into my life, I've eaten fattier foods in larger volumes than I have in years." I stood and started clearing the dishes. "You three will cause *me* to gain weight!"

"You look great from where I'm standing." Gray's words were smooth, and I blushed.

"Stop, you're going to give me a big head." I walked

into the kitchen to escape the compliment lingering in the air. The three men were dead silent. Curiosity got the better of me, and I peeked out. They were determinedly looking away from each other. Each one appeared to be fighting off laughter. "What's with you guys?" The humor of the situation flew over my head.

The roar of laughter that met my question left me confused. I opted not to push it anymore and chalked it up to the inside jokes of a long-term friendship. The only guy I'd ever known who wasn't confusing was Todd, but he was more feminine than I was.

Once the laughter died down a bit, I continued clearing the table. Gray took the plates from my hands. "You cooked a wonderful dinner, Hermosa. Let us do the cleanup."

"Stop. The host cleans, that's how it is. We *are* still in the South, aren't we?"

"Hush." Arch chided me. "That's not how *we* work. Our families all had the same rule: The cook doesn't clean. You cooked, we clean."

Three sets of eyes stared me down until I relinquished the plates. "Okay, okay!" I laughed. "You win. Enjoy the chores. Rubber gloves and dish soap are under the sink if you need to hand wash anything. Dishwasher detergent is in the cabinet above the dishwasher. Good luck figuring out where all my clean dishes go."

I didn't mind them poking around in my kitchen. There was nothing in there to be embarrassed about.

My favorite gossip magazine waited on my coffee

table, woefully ignored. I plopped down on my comfy sofa to engross myself in mindless drivel. Satan jumped up beside me, purring. The magazine held little appeal, however, compared to the conversation and laughter coming from my kitchen.

"Dude, have you ever done dishes before? You can't put those in the dishwasher." Arch's deep voice penetrated the silence in the living room.

Gray did something nonverbal because I heard a snort before he replied, "Shut up. Dishwasher commercials are misleading. It's unlikely anything except the worst baked-on food needs to be pre-washed."

The sound of the cabinets opening and closing covered up Wes's response, but I soon heard Arch again. "I can't believe we ate all of the lasagna. I feel bad. What if she wanted leftovers?"

It sounded like Gray threw the dishes in the sink, if the loud splash and Wes's subsequent yelp were any indication. "Nah, this was supposed to be a date. You two are intruders."

"Are you mad? She said she cleared it with you first." Arch's voice sounded a bit hesitant as if he wasn't sure he wanted to know the answer.

Wes laughed. "Not at all, I'm messing with you. I'm saying she probably made this meal with the intention of having leftovers all week since it was originally the two of us."

He nailed it. I had, in fact, looked forward to not cooking dinner, even if only for a few days. Finals week quickly approached, and any extra time I could get in studying was valuable. There was silence for a few moments with only the sounds of feet shuffling. Satan began to knead his paws on my lap.

The guys worked in companionable silence. My mind wandered and soon I imagined what it would be like to be in a serious relationship with each of the hunky guys. I searched for pros and cons with each, but I couldn't get past the pros. Of course, there was the obvious con. I was attracted to all three of them.

"Why don't we make her a casserole and bring it to her in the morning. That way, if she wants leftovers, she'll have some." Gray's hushed voice brought me out of my musings. They were trying to stay quiet and surprise me, but sound carried in my apartment.

"Great idea." I barely heard Arch's muffled voice. "We need to find out if she likes Mexican. We can make her tortilla casserole."

Gray sounded offended. "C'mon, man. That's not Mexican food. It's what Americans *think* is Mexican food."

Wes replied defensively. "It's still good."

Gray sighed. "Yeah... It is."

The dishwasher turned on, and I lost track of the conversation. I couldn't wait to see what casserole concoction they came up with and how they surprised me with it.

When the dishes were done and the kitchen spick and span, the guys came out, and I got a hug from each of them. Hugging them in front of each other was awkward, especially when Wes kissed me on the cheek again. Once I waved them out the door, I washed my face, brushed my teeth, and got into bed with a goofy smile on my face.

The next morning, as I heated a bagel, a knock rang through my apartment. There was a definite spring in my step as I ran across the living room. I'd already practiced my surprised face for when they dropped off the casserole.

I jerked open the door to find my stepbrother standing in the hall. "I have *got* to start checking my security system!" I almost shouted at him.

"We need to talk, Ellie. Can I come in?" His thin voice pleaded.

"No." There was nothing to say to him.

"Come on, Ellie. I want to talk to you. We can figure something out and settle this fiasco without any more messiness in court."

Mitch was apologetic and weak. He'd always appeared weak. Weak chin, receding hairline. He was twenty-four and balding. I hoped he lost all his hair by thirty—but only on top. I sighed. "Fine. Come in, but make it quick. I need to get to class." He walked past me smelling of the same overpriced cologne he wore in high school. The stench made me want to gag.

He'd been horrible to me growing up, but it was all underhanded and sneaky. Passive-aggressive horribleness. He'd never done anything bold, and physically, I should be safe enough to allow him in my home.

I let him in. Closing us up in the apartment together made me uncomfortable. I didn't like being alone with him. "What do you want, Mitch?"

He walked past my couch to gaze out the window. Satan jumped off the couch as Mitch passed, growling and hissing. He hid under my dining table.

Gathering his words first, Mitch responded a moment later. I tried to keep my mind from straying to my past.

"Give it up, Ellie. I know you. You can't keep this up." His tone flipped from apologetic to domineering.

"What're you talking about?" I didn't want to know.

"The company. You can't handle running a huge publishing company! You don't know the first thing about being a CEO."

I immediately bristled. He had no right to come into my home and speak to me in that manner. "Get out. I don't have to listen to this crap." I'd lost all familial ties to him and had no reason to put up with his gall.

"I'm not leaving until I talk some sense into you. We were connected as kids. I know you always felt it." He tried to placate me, the fool. The only connection we had as kids was his obsession with putting me down and making me feel like a fat, frumpy fool.

"Connected how? You're crazy." I moved toward my cell phone. I wanted to be able to call Arch if Mitch's words grew any more insane.

"You can't tell me you didn't feel the connection. You're lying if you say it." His breath came more rapidly. I'd never seen him so openly agitated.

"I'm going to need you to give me a little more information. You treated me like a dog for the time we lived under the same roof. How were we connected?" Perhaps he considered breaking my things and leering at my friends a connection?

"Ellie." Mitch's voice started to sound whiny. "It was a forbidden love. We dared not explore it. But now, our parents aren't married anymore! We don't have anything holding us back." My brain refused to work. Once the word love came out of his mouth, I went into shock and denial.

My eyes couldn't have opened wider if an optometrist used his special tools to do it. My mouth gaped open; I couldn't believe what I was hearing. "Forbidden? Love?"

"You were attracted to me. At first, I wasn't attracted to you, but your grace—poise—I was drawn to you. And knowing you returned my affections... I used to ache for you if I brought home a date. I didn't want you to imagine I cared any less for you because I was keeping up pretenses. But we're free now, Ellie. Free!" I didn't process nearly everything he said. As his voice rose in pitch, it reminded me of prepubescent Mitch, ripping pages out of my favorite books—books my mother gave me—and leaving them under my covers.

My mouth wouldn't form words. He took it as permission to continue. "I can get my mom to give me the company if you give up your claim." He moved away from the window to stand between the entryway and me. I regretted walking away from my only exit. He cut off my escape route.

My emotions bounced from irritation to anger to

panic, but mostly anger. After I tried for years to separate myself from him, I was angry he was still a stressor in my life. I was irritated I'd allowed him to come between the door and me. And I was panicked because I didn't know what he was capable of if he believed the insanity coming out of his mouth. "Then we can get married, and you can help. You can plan the events and host dinner parties. Like my mom did for your dad. It'll be the ideal arrangement. And our children would be perfect, Ellie, think about it!" He'd gone off the deep end.

The mention of children—and what I'd have to do with him to *get* those children—shook me out of my stupor. "Children?" I asked, incredulous. "Married? Dinner parties? Oh. My. *God*!" By the time the second 'god' left my lips, I was shrieking. "Get out of my house, you sicko!"

"Ellie, what's wrong with you?" He definitely crossed into the land of whining.

"What's wrong with me?" My voice, quiet and deep, dropped its shriek. Danger ran through my veins. He had to leave my presence before I lost it and ended up in jail. "What's wrong with *you*? I never had forbidden feelings for you, you perverted weasel."

"Why are you being hurtful about our love? We were kids. There's nothing perverted about how kids feel, they can't help their growing emotions and attractions." He inched toward me.

"Hurtful? I'm being hurtful?" My eyes darted around the room, trying to find an escape.

"Why do you keep repeating everything I say?" His voice turned superior.

"Because I can't believe the words coming out of your mouth! Who are you? You can't be the boy I grew up with. You were *horrible* to me!" Images flashed through my mind. Years of verbal abuse and bullying. Taunts about everything from my hair to my weight. The barrage of hate Todd also endured on his visits. This was all compounded by the actions of his group of so-called cool friends, who blindly imitated their leader.

"That was a ruse! You had to have known. I kept up pretenses so no one would figure out our true feelings." He pleaded with me to understand his side. The only side I could understand was he'd gone completely insane.

"Mitch, get out! Get out! *Get out!*" With each repetition, my voice rose in pitch until I screamed at him, and I didn't care.

"I'm not leaving, Ellie! You must admit you care for me. I can't leave until you admit it!" Now, Mitch screamed at me.

"I hate you. With a burning passion, I hate you. I never thought I could hate anyone until I met you and your family. And now, I hate you more because you're stark, raving *insane*, and you won't get the hell out of my apartment!" My eyes darted, searching for a way around him. He was too close.

He started walking toward me again. His eyes were crazed, and I could see sweat beading on his overly large forehead. "Don't come any closer, you...you..." I searched for another appropriate word. "Pervert!"

"My patience wears thin, *sister*." He grew angrier, which scared me to death. He was unpredictable, totally off his rocker, nothing like the boy I knew. "Stop calling me crazy. I didn't imagine our flirtations. I didn't invent you staring at me across the room, lust in your eyes. You were a little young to have steamy thoughts about me, but since we didn't act on them, there was no harm."

I had no words for the idiocy spewing out of his mouth. "Those weren't lustful thoughts. They were murderous, they were angry." He started toward me again. I put my hands in front of me in the universal stop gesture. "Don't come any closer, Mitch, I mean it!"

He rushed at me and put his arms around my waist before I could flinch. He pushed me against the half wall separating the kitchen from the living room. "You can't deny me, Ellie. We're meant to be. Our future will be perfect together." His fervent attempts to kiss my neck broke his words apart.

Screams ripped from my throat the moment he touched me. I tried to fight him off, but I'd never gotten any real self-defense training. I always meant to. And though I owned a gun for home protection, it was all the way across the room.

I managed to get my knee into his groin, putting him on the ground, but not before he touched me in too many places. I slid along the wall to get around him and ran for the exit.

I screamed my way across the room, mostly

incoherent sentences about Mitch's insanity. When I opened the door, I found Arch in the hall, panic on his face. I ran straight into his arms and instantly calmed in his safe embrace.

"What's going on? What's wrong? I heard you screaming from my apartment!" He sounded frantic. I couldn't imagine the scenarios running through his mind.

"He's crazy! He's in my apartment, and he's crazy!" I began to cry, overwhelmed by the madness of the morning.

Arch disentangled himself from my arms long enough to stick his head into my apartment and see Mitch struggling to rise. "Who the hell is that?"

"My stepbrother, Mitch. Please don't let him come near me!" Screams trapped in my throat. I didn't want Arch to let go.

"Go to my apartment and lock up behind you. I'll take care of Mitch."

"Don't hurt him." I didn't want Arch to get in any trouble. I didn't care if he hurt Mitch.

"I won't. I'm going to call the police to pick him up. He assaulted you?" I nodded my head.

Arguments against calling the police ran through my head but left when Mitch suddenly appeared in the hall. I jumped and ran for Arch's apartment.

I pressed my ear against the door once I got it locked and tried to listen to what they said. They weren't speaking loudly—all I heard was muffled talking.

A loud thud rattled the wood against my ear, causing

me to jump. I pressed my eye to the peephole, hoping I could see what happened. Arch had Mitch pressed up against the wall with one arm across his chest. Mitch, the pantywaist, didn't even try to resist. Through the distorted image, I couldn't tell if he'd given up or if he was overpowered and biding his time.

I didn't dare open the door. Arch could handle himself fine. Besides, seeing me could put Mitch further into a frenzy. I kept watching as building security ran into view and handcuffed Mitch.

Arch knocked on the door. "Let me in, I want to make sure you're okay." I unlocked the door and slammed it shut behind him, re-locking it as fast as I could. He put his arms around me again, and I basked in his warmth. I focused on the smell of his aftershave. Breathe in and out. "Joe, the guard, has him subdued, and if he tries to run, he won't get far in cuffs. The police should be here any minute. I pressed your panic button on your alarm system. Why didn't you press it?"

My mind was fuzzy. "I didn't suspect I was in any danger at first. Then, I got mad at myself for letting him cut off my escape. I spent what feels like a ridiculous amount of time being worried about why I'd never taken the self-defense classes I've always wanted to take." I snuggled in closer to him without consideration for the intimacy of the moment. "My thoughts didn't make much sense through the whole encounter."

"That's understandable." Arch squeezed me tighter. His arms became my security. He only let me go to answer the door for the police.

"Thank you for coming, officers." An older male walked in, followed by a younger female.

"No problem. The intruder has been taken to the station. We need some information from you." I spent the next twenty minutes explaining my convoluted relationship with Mitch and how he'd crossed the line in my apartment.

As I began to describe Mitch's behavior in my apartment, Todd rushed into the room in a bright floral silk robe and red house slippers. Every eye turned away from me. I appreciated a moment to breathe before recounting the narrative.

Todd sat on one side and Arch on the other. They swathed me in love and security to tell my scary tale. Gray and Wes walked in before I finished and heard the tail end of my fiasco. When I'd said all I could, the lawyers and the officers talked shop in the hall for a moment, and finally left me alone with my friends, new and old.

"What in the world happened?" Wes asked.

"I don't have the energy to go through it again." I leaned against Todd, exhausted. "Arch, Todd, you heard me tell it. Can you please fill them in?" I closed my eyes and tried to concentrate on the fact that three gorgeous guys—and gorgeous Todd, of course—were utterly interested in my well-being, and not because I paid them to be. I listened to the murmur of their voices until I drifted to sleep.

CHAPTER TEN

When I woke, Todd had gone, and I slept alone on the sofa, comfy on a plush pillow. "I can't believe Todd left, and you put a pillow under my head, and I slept through it all." I was shaky from a nightmare about Mitch. The nightmare was a barrage of memories, combining this morning's horror with the pain and bullying of my youth. "Did I talk in my sleep again?"

Gray, nestled into a recliner, watched me wake up with a smile on his face. "Good morning, sleepyhead. You did talk, a little. I sat beside you and rubbed your head, and it seemed to soothe you." I must've slept hard. It meant a lot that he'd stay and care for me.

I sat up and tried to get my brain to wake to a functional level. Glancing around the room, I found it empty. "What time is it? Where did everyone go?" My heavy heart, still reeling from the nightmare thumped painfully in my chest. I rubbed the goose bumps on my arms.

"Arch and Wes went to the office to try to get some work done. Todd left first, mumbling something about too much testosterone. I'm your protector for the day." He checked his phone. "And it's eleven."

"No! I missed my morning class. I need to go email my professor." What a fantastic way to show my professors how responsible I was before they might have to give a deposition.

"Missing one class isn't that big of a deal. Don't sweat it."

"I do sweat it, considering we're in a fight for my future and my professors will make up a huge chunk of my case—and, I missed time the other day because of the wreck." I didn't mean to sound accusatory, but I didn't want to give my stepmother any ammo.

"I'm not a civil law expert, of course, but I'd imagine once they present the evidence of your stepbrother's insanity to the court, this day will only help your case. Your stepmother planned on giving him a position in the company." He paused, then added, "That's not legal advice. It's a guess."

I nodded along and smiled at his disclaimer. "I'm sure you're right, but I would've preferred almost any other way to discover that." I shuddered, the remnants of the nightmare still lingering in my brain.

"Do you have any other classes today?" Gray abruptly changed the subject.

"No, I've got a light course load this semester." I threw my head against the pillow and put one arm over my eyes, still overwhelmed.

"Then it's me and you until dinner, doll. What's your poison?"

"Goodness, I wasn't expecting an impromptu date. What do you think?" I peeked at him from under my arm.

"I'm putty in your hands, gorgeous." Gray winked, making my stomach do little flips, which gave me an idea of how we could start our day. A distraction from my nerves.

"You know what I'd like? I'd like to watch you do a wall flip, and then see your comic book collection."

"You want all that, huh?" He swallowed, exaggerated... like I made him nervous.

"I sure do." I threw my arms out and jumped up from my spot on the couch. "This day is looking up." I forced the last remnants of the nightmare to the back of my mind.

"I believe I can oblige. Come on." He opened the door for me.

"Let me stop in and get my stuff." I rattled the door to my apartment. Locked, and my keys were inside. I stared at my bare feet and sighed. "Let's go get the building manager. Todd is in class. No getting a key from him now."

The ride down the elevator was hilarious. Gray distracted me from my embarrassment over my bare feet by pretending to speak into his suit jacket cuff like a secret agent. When the elderly grouch from the fourth floor got on, he whispered to his wrist. "Target confirmed. Our position is ideal. Don't engage, I'll handle this myself. Target is hostile. Blue shirt, pearls." Old Ms. Grouchy wore a blue blouse and fat pearls.

I barely contained my laughter as she squinted down at her shirt then fingered her pearls. She tried to surreptitiously sneak a peek behind her at Gray, to see who he was and why he was talking like that. As soon as she glanced back he straightened, put his arms at his side, and stared straight ahead like a soldier.

We reached the ground floor, and she shot out of the elevator faster than she'd probably moved in a decade. I let the elevator sit there for a moment while I composed myself. "You almost made me pee, Gray! You scared that poor, old woman to death."

"Mission accomplished," he whispered into his cuff. When I could breathe again, we exited the elevator and found the manager in his office. Gray waited in the hall.

"Good morning, Mr. Simpson. Could I get a copy of my apartment key? I'll bring it right back." I smiled at the lanky man.

He eyeballed my feet before chuckling. "Of course, Ms. Asche. Coming up." He kept the keys stored by last name in a locked filing cabinet. I was the first name in the files and had the key in my hand in no time.

As I turned to join Gray in the hall, Mr. Simpson stopped me. "Ms. Asche, why don't you go ahead and put your mother on your list of allowed visitors. If she ever leaves her key at home again, I'll be able to lend her one, too."

My body froze, fear lacing up and down my spine. "My mother?"

"Yeah. Ms. Reynolds, I think it was? Nice lady. I'm sorry I couldn't let her in the other day, but rules are rules. And after what happened with your attacker today, it's even more important we be diligent."

I stopped, shocked by his words. My mother? He noticed my reaction, as he rubbed his balding head, unsure of himself.

"As to the attacker, I was going to stop by later and check in on you, but I was trying to figure out how I should approach you. I'm sorry this happened to you." His facial expression edged with panic. "We're working diligently to figure out how he got in the building. The codes have been recently changed. He either knew how to hack the system, or someone gave him a code." He sighed. "The company that built the system is taking this personally. They're trying to figure out what happened."

I took pity on him, miserable that something of that magnitude happened on his watch. "I appreciate that very much. And thank you for your apology. But, you should know, my mother died when I was eight."

I chose my next words carefully. "I do have a stepmother, but she shouldn't ever be given a key nor be allowed entry. The same goes for anyone else claiming to be related to me. You absolutely did the right thing denying her, and I'm grateful. I wonder though, how did *she* get in the building? The doorman wouldn't let anyone in without the appropriate codes, and the entrances otherwise have keypads. Could she have had access to the same code used today?"

Mr. Simpson blinked rapidly, stunned. "I didn't realize. I assumed she had your code. I'll add this to the information to give the alarm company for their research."

"Mr. Simpson, if necessary, would you be willing to give a statement that you refused her entry to my apartment?" He looked uneasy. "Also, would there happen to be any security camera footage?"

He shuffled his feet behind his desk. "I hate to tell you this, especially after the problem with the codes, but our lobby cameras were on the fritz that day. We got them fixed right after she left. The only way we'd have footage is if she happened to go upstairs and tried to get in. Those cameras were working fine."

"I'd be grateful to you if you'd check for me," I said. What rotten luck.

"Of course, I will." He nodded his head.

I smiled one last time and headed out.

We made our way to my apartment to get my shoes, and I told Gray what I learned. He insisted I call Mr. Kohl to fill him in, which I did as we walked down to his SUV. After explaining what happened, I asked, "What'll this mean for my case?"

"At best, we can have her arrested for attempted breaking and entering. She tried to lie to gain entry to your home. At worst, there'll be absolutely no video footage, and she'll get someone to give her an alibi, and it won't mean squat," Mr. Kohl replied. "Even if she's arrested, it may or may not help the case, as this is a civil case and that would be a criminal matter."

"Here's to hoping they got something on camera." After hanging up, I spent a few minutes reflecting on how my dad got looped in by such a horrible woman.

A reporter lurked outside the building's front door. Thanks to the anonymity of the Explorer, he ignored us as we pulled out of the garage.

"Hey. Snap out of it. I'm sure they're building up plenty of evidence. You got this." Gray grinned at me out of the side of his mouth as he concentrated on the road. His confidence heartened me, and I had to admit it did wonders to soothe some of my nervousness. As did his smile.

"I'm okay. Wondering what I did in a past life to get stuck with her." I didn't deserve someone so horrible.

Gray let out a wry chuckle. "You must've done something pretty bad. Did you make it a habit to go around kicking kittens? Or insulting deities?"

I rolled my eyes at his attempt at humor, but also tucked my lip under my teeth to keep from smiling. "What're we going to do at your place?"

His eyes lit up. "I thought you'd never ask! What do you know about comic books?"

My brows furrowed a slight bit. "I know a little from the superhero movies. I love watching superhero movies." As an afterthought, I threw out, "Capes are a definite turn on."

"I'll log that one away for future reference," he said with a straight face. "Any other preferences, besides capes?"

My giggles gave me away before I even said the words. "I love a man in tights."

"I'll find the pictures of Wes in his Peter Pan costume. They're stashed somewhere for future blackmail." He couldn't hide the laughter in his voice.

Giggles soon turned to belly laughs. The short drive to his apartment building was fun instead of a worry-fest about my stepfamily. Gray had a knack for cracking me up.

Gray's apartment building wasn't as nice as mine, but it also wasn't a hovel. "Have you lived here long?"

"Since we moved from Atlanta after college to start the firm." Ever the gentleman, he jumped out and ran around to open my door before I could even get my seatbelt off and pick up my purse.

"You're awfully young to have such a successful firm. How'd you do it?"

"We started college at sixteen, thanks to homeschooling. Finished at twenty-three." He shrugged like it was no big deal. "When we first started, we all shared the apartment I live in now. We were broke, living off a small allowance from our parents."

He opened the door to an elevator alcove. "They gave us six months to start making our own money before they cut us off. We lasted another six months on small nickel and dime cases. Luckily, we won most of them." He tapped the six buttons.

"What changed?"

"A man came to us, said he was innocent. He was accused of murder, and the prosecution's case was strong."

"You believed him?" They were ballsy to take on such a difficult case.

"He convinced us. We aren't about defending criminals. We'll defend someone if we believe their innocence. He was the first, though."

"I take it you won the case?" I was impressed.

"Sure did. We worked around the clock searching for loopholes, previous cases. We ended up catching a break by figuring out he had a brother that had been put up for adoption as an infant."

The elevator dinged, and we got out. "The brother framed him for the murder. Said he planned to take over the guy's life, the life he should've had all along."

"That sounds like a story out of a thriller novel." I should commission the story.

"Doesn't it? It was a miracle we happened upon the only surviving document from the sealed adoption and were curious enough to go down that rabbit hole."

"So, you got a lot of media attention?" I asked as I followed him down the sixth floor hallway.

"Tons. The entire world heard about the case. Everyone in our city was so convinced he was guilty. When the truth came out, the public hailed him a hero. They even had a parade for him. You don't get outcomes like that one often."

We stopped, and he pulled out a key. "After his case,

every criminal in the city called us to defend them. We have to screen defendants carefully. We put them through a rigorous interviewing process."

His apartment was decorated like mine—that is to say, it was hardly decorated at all. He had bare, cream-colored walls and boring, forgettable furniture. "You don't spend much time here, do you?" I asked.

Only one framed picture hung on the wall. I got close enough to realize it was his own diploma, in a frame similar to Arch's, and also held a picture of his family.

He glanced around. "Actually, no. I do sleep here, but I'm renovating a place outside the city where I spend a large portion of my free time." A proud grin plastered on his face.

"Hey, Arch has this same frame. This is your family?" He smiled and nodded. The picture showed a large family. Three women and a man stood behind him, and eight children ranging from baby to teen surrounded them. "You've got quite the extended family, Gray *Baron*. You and Arch have such regal names."

He grunted, uncomfortable with talk about his family. I changed the subject. "How far is the house you're renovating?" It couldn't have been far, unless he stopped going recently. Since the day we met, it seemed like he was always within arm's reach.

"About thirty minutes from here." I followed him into the kitchen where he grabbed a couple bottles of water. The kitchen was decorated like the living room—bare. "I haven't been out there since before I met you though, there's too much going on with our current case. That's the way of it. When I'm done with the case, I probably won't take another one for a few weeks. I'll use that time to go play at the house for a while." He handed me a bottle.

"Are you renovating it by yourself?" I took a long drink of the cold water. I hadn't had anything to drink since my juice at breakfast.

"Mostly. I'm no good with wiring, so I contract it out. Arch is the plumbing genius. Any plumbing issues wait for him to be able to get out there. Wes is a good all-around handyman; he helps me quite a bit." We returned to the living room as he spoke.

"I'm having the hardest time imagining you three swinging hammers and installing pipes! I need to see for myself."

"We'll all go out some weekend soon. You can tour my dream home. It's where I hope to raise kids one day." His voice was low and excited. His future family meant a lot to him.

"Sounds great. I'm in." I began to imagine how gorgeous little Ellie and Gray babies would be. *Oh, no. No babies yet.* I didn't even know where they came from. I couldn't even choose a guy; I certainly couldn't be entertaining the idea of starting a family with one. "I'm in for a date. Not the kids. I want kids, but…" *Shut up, Ellie.* "I'm going to stop talking now." My face burned bright red.

Gray busted out laughing. "Cool." He changed the

subject. "Come over here and behold the marvel of my comic collection." I snickered at his pun while he opened the door to a spare bedroom filled with tables. Meticulously labeled boxes with what universe, book, and issues they contained lined the tables.

I opened the closest box to find a man dressed in a black costume. He had lots of muscles and fought a man dressed in purple. "I know this one! I've seen a lot of these movies. They're good."

"He's one of my favorite characters. Feel free to browse the boxes. I'm going to go change into something more comfortable since I won't be going to work today." I barely noticed him leave the room. I was engrossed in reading the sides of the boxes for any other reference I recognized.

I found several and was three pages into one about my favorite superhero movie when he returned. He changed into a red and black flannel shirt, dark boot-cut jeans, and black motorcycle boots. His hair was still pulled back and braided. He looked like a cowboy biker. I mentally ordered my jaw not to hit the floor.

I forced my eyes to the comic. I didn't want to be accused of staring. The words and pictures on the page blurred as I snuck another glance. He turned away from me and rifled through one of the boxes. The view from behind was even better. I took a deep breath and faced away to remove the temptation to stare.

"Something wrong? You sighed."

"Nope! No. I'm fine. Just fine. Reading about, uh, this

one here..." My words faltered as he walked around to my front. His elusive tattoo peeked from beneath his shirt.

He peered into my eyes and put his hands on my arms. His eyes moved to his watch. "Crap. I didn't even think about how late it is. I bet you're starving. Let's order some lunch."

"Sure! Sounds good." My voice, too high and cheerful, didn't sound like me. I couldn't stop peeking at his biceps under the flannel material. I'd never been a shallow person, at least I didn't like to think I was, but if Gray dressed like a cowboy biker all the time, I'd definitely have a harder time choosing. I'd be hooked. *He said they all prefer flannels. Oh, hell.* A hormone-riddled teenager would've had better control. Being around all the sexy man hotness messed with my maturity levels.

We moved into the living room, and he pulled a file folder out of a desk drawer in the corner. "I've got menus for anything you can imagine. Being downtown, everyone delivers. What sounds good?"

"Anything, really. Subs, Chinese, Mexican, you name it." My stomach rumbled.

"If you want Mexican, I'll cook for you one day soon. My mother was born in Mexico. I can cook better than most of the restaurants in town."

"Mmmm, sounds heavenly. My dad loved authentic Mexican food, and I do, too. He always told my mom he was lucky she *wasn't* Mexican, because if she were, he'd weigh three hundred pounds. Then she'd slap him and make him tamales."

"I won't try to beat your mom's tamale recipe." He chuckled. "We'll make a different authentic Mexican dish one day. How does chicken mole sound?"

"Perfect." We picked out a sub shop and ordered sandwiches and chips. While we waited, I snooped through his Netflix watch list and found many of the same shows on my own queue. He wasn't a big book reader like Wes, but we could at least watch a TV show together.

We'd both been binge watching the same show about a group of female prisoners. After our lunch, we spent the rest of the afternoon watching the latest episodes. The show contained a significant amount of adult content, and I blushed several times in the course of the afternoon. Watching a lustful scene with my potential boyfriend in the room ate at my nerves.

One particularly uncomfortable scene caused me to peek at Gray out of the corner of my eye, curious if he felt as awkward as I did. When I realized he was giving me the side eye, I started to giggle.

"What's wrong with you?" Gray laughed at me when I couldn't reply because of my giggles. He paused the TV. "Is this show too much for you?"

Once I quieted down, I realized he'd moved close to me. "No! I love it. I've never watched such a racy show with someone I…" I trailed off. "You know what? Never mind, I'm fine." My smile was forced and wooden. I did *not* want to explain myself.

"Someone you what?" he asked.

"Someone I'm attracted to." There, I said it. I hoped

he was happy.

"Was that so hard to say?"

I pouted and turned up my nose. "A little, yeah."

A calloused finger touched my protruding bottom lip. I turned to face Gray. His face moved close to mine—so close, it was an effort to focus my eyes. My gaze moved from his cognac eyes to his full lips, and my breath caught. The room was silent as my stomach filled with delicious anticipation.

A sizzle started in my chest the moment Gray's lips met mine. My body tightened. Our mouths met for a moment before he pulled back and met my gaze. I closed my eyes to savor the moment and let out a small purr.

The small sound I made caused a visceral reaction in Gray. He grabbed my shoulders with firm, yet gentle hands, and crushed my lips to his. I opened my mouth to breathe, and he took advantage of my lips parting. His tongue flicked across my bottom lip. I tentatively stuck my tongue out to touch his. My nerves got the better of me, so I pulled my tongue back and closed my mouth. I pressed my hands on his chest. I didn't want to get too carried away.

He rested his forehead against mine and pressed another closed-mouth kiss to my lips. "You kiss like fire. I shouldn't play with fire," he whispered.

"I won't burn you," I lied. I still didn't know which of the three men to choose. If Gray grew attached and I didn't do the same, he could get burned. "Tell me about your tattoo." I asked, eyes on the bit of it that peeked out of his shirt.

To my consternation, he unbuttoned his shirt, slowly revealing his tatted chest. My lungs began to burn and a quiver started in a place I wasn't ready to feel a quiver in. It was too soon for quivers. He removed his shirt completely while I stared at a massive scales of justice, complete with a snake twining around the sword. "It's beautiful."

I ran my fingers tentatively along the blade of the sword, straight down Grays' chest. Goosebumps erupted all over his torso. I stared up into his dark eyes and exhaled through my nose.

It had been years since I'd been to bed with a man. He would surely treat me gently, respectfully, and lovingly, but I'd never jumped straight into bed with a man. *You're not starting now.* I tried to look anywhere other than his toned chest or deep eyes, but couldn't do it.

"I need to go," I whispered. "I'm doing a tutoring session tonight at the GED testing center."

He leaned in for one last soft kiss before buttoning his shirt up. "You've got a lot going on."

I sighed as his chest and tattoo disappeared. "I don't mind it. There's plenty of time to slow down later in life. And, I don't work full time like a lot of other students. It's not as bad as it seems." I sometimes battled guilt about how easy I had it. I wanted to help other people have it a little easier.

Gray smiled down at me. "You're something special, Ellie. I'll take you home."

"Thank you," I replied, a little uncomfortable with the compliment. "I had a wonderful afternoon."

"So did I. I was glad to be your watchdog today."

While Gray turned out the lights and got ready to leave, I texted Todd to ask if he and Rick would stay in my guest room for the night. I wasn't ready to be alone after the nightmare with Mitch.

I pondered my situation the entire way home. What was I getting myself into? Was *I* playing with fire? How badly could I get burned? I didn't know the answers to these questions. And I was afraid to find out.

CHAPTER ELEVEN

The next two weeks were a blur. Todd and I had finals, and though I had a light course load, the professors demanded excellence. High scores were crucial to passing the classes with good grades. I managed to maintain a 4.0 GPA, and I didn't want to lose momentum.

Finals week was all the more difficult by Mitch-centered nightmares appearing nightly. I started going to my therapist again. With the help of therapy, I worked through all my childhood emotional traumas, but the Mitch encounter effectively demolished the thousands of dollars of work done to my psyche.

My three potential suitors managed to find ways to make finals week less overwhelming, even belatedly producing the secret casserole. At the same time, they further confused and attracted me. They sent sweet texts wishing me luck, slipped handwritten notes under my apartment door, left care packages outside my door including bananas—brain food—coffee shop gift cards, puzzle books for taking breaks, and my favorite gum. All of which baffled me. After a lifetime of flying under the radar, as well as the residual effects of my stepfamily's influence, I worked hard to deal gracefully and appreciatively with the sudden onslaught of attention and care.

The hidden benefit of the hectic weeks was while my lawyers did their thing and got my case ready, I was distracted by school, volunteering, and the three guys rotating in and out of my days. They took turns showing they cared about me, even though they spent plenty of time working on their case. I frequently forgot my nervousness about the trial as the first of the year approached. I'd have plenty of time to fret over winter break.

Gray made sure I didn't cook dinner a single time during my studying and test-taking binges. He enlisted Todd's advice, and every evening when I returned from class or the library, I found a delicious meal ready to heat up.

My favorites were the simpler ones such as vegetable beef soup, chili, and burgers. A few times when I walked in—brain fried—he stood in my kitchen cooking. Those nights he made something more complicated. His presence threw me the first time I walked in to an apartment that wasn't empty, but once I learned he was there with Todd's permission, I relaxed and enjoyed the pampering.

I liked to tease him for making fancy dinners—things like stuffed pork chops, filet mignon, and I finally tried his chicken mole. I was in heaven, except for the calorie count. He assured me he used fresh, organic, low calorie ingredients whenever possible to cut down on calories. The three of them treated healthy eating like a lifestyle choice, which I appreciated. There was nothing obsessive about it, but good choices were made.

Wes showed he cared about my stress levels through books. Several mornings I woke to find a new edition of his favorite series sitting in the hall. He started me on book one, and by the time I finished my finals, I had five.

It was an addicting series, and I couldn't wait to dive into them and connect further with Wes. I stole a little time along the way and managed to read the first book. It was torture, forcing myself to wait until winter break to begin the next.

Arch relieved tension simply by being present. He must've watched constantly for me to come home every night; because not long after I set my stuff down, he came knocking to check on me. A few times he brought a small gift to show he cared, even though I didn't have quality time to spare. He also took on Satan duties. He played with him, fed him, and took care of his litter box. The poor kitty didn't even notice my neglect thanks to Arch.

Perhaps my favorite thing they did, however, was when Arch took on all my volunteer shifts at the animal shelter. It was a relief to know the animals would be taken care of without trying to juggle time there. He enjoyed it so much, he ended up signing up for shifts of his own for the rest of the year. I was proud to share the rewarding experience with him.

The bubble bath set was a thoughtful gift, as well. Once Gray's delicious cooking filled my belly, I grabbed one of the books given to me by Wes and relaxed in a bubble bath provided by Arch, ready to recharge and hit the books again the next day.

Todd was a jealous mess throughout our finals. Rick was still in the middle of a nasty audit at his accounting firm and couldn't give much support. I mentioned it to Arch in passing. After that, my gifts and food often included enough for two. I had a sneaking suspicion Todd also began to get deliveries of his own books and bubble baths. With a little pressing, he admitted he was also on the receiving end of their generosity.

Finally, gloriously, my finals weeks concluded. The first two weeks of December disappeared, and I had four weeks to spend time with my new friends, Todd and Rick, and search for any angle I could to help me win my company.

We celebrated the end of the dreaded tests by going out. Friday afternoon, I got a text from Wes as I left the last exam of the semester.

Wes: Are you finished yet?

I couldn't contain my excitement, even in a text.

Ellie: I'M ALL DONE!

Wes: Excellent! We want to take you out to celebrate. Dancing?

If only he knew.

Ellie: Absolutely. What time?

Wes: We'll pick you up at six. Bring Todd and Rick.

Immediately, I relayed the information to Todd, and his excitement level matched mine. We made plans to get ready before the guys arrived. Rick would roll his eyes, as he did when we danced, but secretly he loved to watch Todd in his element.

I got home late in the morning and took a leisurely nap. I crawled under the covers and succumbed to blissful sleep.

What seemed like moments later, I felt a continuous nudge against my side, and my eyes opened, blinking rapidly as they adjusted to the light. Todd stood above me, hand on his hip and frowned pointedly at his watch. Time to get ready.

"Giving you the key to this apartment was the best idea I ever had," I said. "I don't have to wake up to a jarring doorbell or alarm. I just wait for you to come in." I stretched and smiled appreciatively. "You spoil me."

He rolled his eyes. "I adore you, of course I spoil you. Now, get your lazy ass up, and take a shower."

"Yes, sir!" I did as directed and hopped in the shower. By then, I was aware of what sort of soaps, lotions, conditioners, and exfoliators I should use. He didn't have to give many directions.

I was about done shaving my legs when Todd strolled in the bathroom. "You're taking forever."

"Sorrrrry," I said, voice dripping sarcasm. "We've got

an hour and a half."

"I still have to get ready, too. I'm looking forward to a date night with Rick!" I couldn't see him standing outside the shower, but I could tell by the sound of his voice he was preening.

"You still have to give me at least one dance. We'll show them what we can do," I said.

"Of course!" The sounds of little pots and creams being moved around filled the bathroom as he rustled around in my makeup. "I'm going to make you ultra-sexy tonight. Those boys will be falling all over themselves."

I rinsed my legs. "Stay on this side of sexy, and not *that* side—slutty."

Todd let out a maniacal laugh. "Whatever you say, my pet."

As I turned off the water and stepped out of the shower, Todd held open a warmed, oversized towel. I took a moment to luxuriate in the heat as it wrapped around me. "This is wonderful!"

"It's not to spoil you, let me assure you. The warm towel will keep your pores open. When you apply this lotion, it'll absorb all the better." He put a bottle of scented cream in my hand and waltzed out of the bathroom.

"Love you, too!" I called out behind him.

I hated it when he was right. When I finished, my skin was like velvet. As I entered my bedroom in my robe, I wasn't prepared for the gorgeous blue dress hanging from one of my curtain rods. "Todd!" I gasped. "Where'd it come from?"

"I shopped while you were taking your power nap." His unexpected voice behind me made me jump. He was in my closet, doing...whatever Todd did in the closet. He kept enough clothes for me in there to keep him busy for a week.

Reminding myself it wouldn't look good to the judge if I killed my best friend, no matter how justifiable, I took a deep breath and stated firmly, "Ok. That's it. Tomorrow afternoon, we're boxing up a ton of those clothes and donating them."

"Yeah, you're right. It's time." His words agreed, but his voice conveyed grudging acceptance.

"We can donate all the fancy dresses to The Glass Slipper project. They lend them to underprivileged girls for prom dresses."

Todd's eyes lit up. "I love the idea! And there's another organization that takes business clothes for the homeless. They wear them for interviews. We'll call them, too!"

I suddenly had an even better idea. "You know what I want to do? Let's go thrift store shopping and buy them out of prom dresses. They'll be sitting there collecting dust this time of year. The thrift store owners will be delighted for the extra income, and the prom places will be happy for all the dresses!"

Todd's smile grew. "I'm in. I love thrift store shopping! Please tell me I get your presence all day? This could take a while." He pushed his hands together, praying to spend time with me.

"All day. Oh, I'm excited. We'll shop tomorrow and go through my clothes Sunday. Then Monday we'll deliver it all. Is Rick still working every day?"

"Yeah, until the New Year. It's all the end of year accounting mess. Then, after the first of the year, they give them extra vacation time to recuperate." His eyes strayed toward the closet. He was dying to go through and pull out clothes to donate.

"Bless his heart. I hope you're taking good care of him." I poked his shoulder to bring him back to our conversation.

"Of course, I am!" Todd said, mock offended. "I spoil him more than I spoil you!"

We continued to banter and plan our shopping weekend while Todd teased my hair into some sort of punk rock up-do, wilder than I'd ever fix for myself. When headed to a club, though, I didn't mind the extra edginess. When he finished my makeup, it was also on the edgy side. Lots of black eyeliner and a bold, red lip. Satan took one peek at me and ran.

Staring into the mirror, I took a critical self-appraisal. "I love it, Todd. You've surprised me. I didn't expect to be pretty with this much extra…stuff."

"You're gorgeous. If you let me dye your hair, it'll make those big eyes and luscious skin pop even more."

Dramatically, I rolled my eyes. "One day. One step at a time."

Todd left me with my dress and heels while he went to

the spare bedroom to get ready. He wanted to play date-night with Rick and go pick him up. Rick always teased him for his romantic antics, but I believed he loved it, too.

The baby blue dress with a black lace overlay on the sleeveless bodice was phenomenal. The skirt stopped at my knee. Any longer and I would've resembled a princess in a cartoon. A silk belt crossed my waist, and the skirt flared when I twirled. I turned on some dancing music and spent several minutes making myself dizzy watching the dress float around me.

To keep it modest, a short pencil skirt hid underneath and stayed close to my body. The tightness of it made me sultry, but at the same time, I'd still be a lady.

I lost track of time as I twirled and admired myself. I glanced up from my beautiful dress and found Todd leaning on the doorframe, watching me. I squealed in surprise. "How long have you been standing there?

"Long enough. I thought you *hated* wearing dresses and skirts?"

"Hush. This dress is amazing, and you know it. I'm allowed to feel like I'm playing dress up when I wear something this fabulous." I smiled prettily and flipped my skirt at him.

Laughter filled the room. "I guess you are."

Suddenly, I wasn't the only one squealing. Arch stood behind Todd. I'd watched him approach, but Todd had no idea. "What in the pits of gay hell?" Todd shouted, voice three octaves too high, as his hand came up to cover his heart.

"Sorry, buddy! I knocked, but I guess you didn't hear it over the music. I tried the handle, and it opened right up." Arch turned to me, lecturing. "Ellie, after what happened with your stepbrother, then your stepmother trying to break in, I'd expect you to be more careful." Arch sounded disappointed in my behavior. The feelings of guilt and shame his words evoked surprised me. His opinion of me had grown enough to make my gut clench at his disappointment.

I tried not to let my emotions show as I attempted to give Arch a wide eyed, innocent stare, but it probably didn't translate well with the eyeliner and punk hair. Todd came to my rescue, though. "I'm the one who left it unlocked, and you're right. With all that's happened, I shouldn't have." He turned to me. "I'm sorry, Ells."

"It's okay, Todd. We aren't used to being paranoid. This is a new, uncomfortable experience for us all." I tried to let Todd off the hook, but I was a little worried he left it unlocked. I'd been fastidious about locking it and setting the security system since the incident with Mitch. The nightmares alone were enough to make me careful. Plus, the building manager had informed me they didn't know where my stepmother or Mitch had gotten access codes. They made the entire building change their security codes again as a precaution.

"Ellie, I'm sorry I didn't say this the second I walked in, but you look amazing." I shivered as Arch's eyes raked up and down my body.

"I'm not finished yet; wait until you see her in the

complete ensemble." Todd gave a fake sniff and wiped at a nonexistent tear as he scurried to my closet. He returned with a pair of silver, strappy heels. The shoes were covered in a clear layer to keep them secure on my feet when dancing. The clear layer was covered in tiny rhinestones, making the shoes appear to be made of glass. "Put these on, and my masterpiece will be complete!"

The tight underskirt of the dress made it more difficult to reach the straps, but I sat dutifully on the bed and began the difficult task of maneuvering them onto my feet.

From the corner of my eye, I watched Arch stride forward. He took the heels from my hand and crouched in front of me. I gawked up at Todd with wide eyes, chills traveling up and down my body. A mass of blazing flames filled my abdomen. Todd made a face while mouthing, "Oh, my dear baby antelopes, *he's putting your shoes on for you*." This statement was punctuated by the O shape of his mouth and his eyebrows dangerously close to vacating the top of his forehead.

Arch ran a finger along my inseam, causing a small snort to erupt from my mouth. He grinned up at me. He knew the effect he had on my body. Behind him, Todd bounced on his toes, nearly clapping in exhilaration. I tried to stop, but the laughter flowed.

With both feet safely ensconced, he placed one hand on my knee and used it to push himself to his feet. His hand lingered there for a moment before he offered it to help me stand.

I heard the snap of a camera and jerked my head up in

time to see Todd lowering his phone. He closed his screen and winked at me. "Picture couldn't have come out more perfect if I tried," he said. "You're a regular fairy tale princess." Arch's cell vibrated before he could comment on the photo taking.

Grabbing his phone, Arch glanced down at the screen before placing it in his jacket pocket. "The guys are downstairs having some difficulties getting in. The codes don't seem to be working again. I'm going to run down there and get them. Meet us down there?" I nodded, and with a wink in my direction, he turned and headed out of the apartment.

I took a few steps to test my stability, growing used to wearing heels; I didn't totter once. I couldn't wait to show off my dancing skills. "Okay, let's go boogie! Finals are over!" I skipped to the front door and flung it open, ready to get the other guys and go to the club.

Stepping into the hallway, I was greeted with a sight I wasn't prepared for. My stepmother found a way around the security again. She stepped off the elevator as Todd came up behind me and put a hand on my waist before he realized who stood in front of me. "Hello, Raquel."

"Ellie." She stared at the hand on my waist. Todd squeezed and gave Raquel a nasty smile.

He spoke for me. "What the hell do you want, Raquel? Why are you here? And how the hell did you get in here, *again*?

If Raquel noticed Todd's emphasis on the last word, she didn't show it.

"I'm here to give you the chance to give up before you ruin your precious lawyers' reputations." Her upper lip curled as she peered past me into my apartment.

"What're you talking about?" Todd was getting angry. I could tell because his hand dug painfully into my side.

"Either you drop your case, or I'll turn you in for the dates you've had with your lawyers, and the time you've spent in their apartments and cars and most likely, their beds. I have photos. I hired a PI." She had an awfully smug expression on her face for someone with a slew of misinformation. I placed my hand on Todd's arm to silence him.

I had an idea, but didn't know if I was brave enough to say it. When her face turned triumphant at my silence, however, I pictured of the guys and what they'd done for me. I found the courage to blurt it out. "That'll be fine. You turn in your photos, and I'll turn in the video I have of you trying to get into my apartment, and the video from the lobby, super's office, elevator, and hallway." Then, remembering what I'd said to the super, "Including today's meeting, as I know you didn't find your way in here with permission."

She blinked at me several times, mulling over my words. "You're bluffing." Her face was impassive, but I knew her mind was in overtime.

"Let's find out." I'd already double checked with Charles—as long as Arch, Wes, and Gray stayed away from my case, we could date. She didn't know it, but she had no leg to stand on.

"Fine. I won't say another word about it. I want you to know you can't win this lawsuit. And I won't destroy my pictures. I'll have them in case I need them."

"We'll see. Now please leave and don't return." Raquel gave me one more ice-bitch glare before whirling and stomping down the hall. I let out the breath I held, and my body relaxed.

Once the elevator doors closed behind her, Todd leaned in to whisper in my ear. "You don't have any video evidence. Your camera system was turned off. And the hallway cameras didn't get a clear shot because of the hat she wore."

"Yes, dear, but *she* doesn't know that. I'm thankful she bought it. We aren't breaking any laws or ethics, but what a pain in the butt it would be if she released her pictures."

"Don't you still need to contact the police department and cancel the charges? They were waiting on video evidence to issue a warrant."

"Hmmm? What did you say?" I asked distractedly. I was celebrating my small victory in my head. I reveled in finally taking the upper hand. "Yeah, I'll do it tomorrow."

I turned to face Todd. He was dashing in a gray, slim-cut suit. I twirled to make my skirt fly and headed for the hallway, grabbing my purse on the way. Todd used his key to lock up behind us, and we went to pick up Rick.

Once there, Todd rapped three times and stood with one hand on his lapel. "You're so debonair," I whispered as the door cracked open. Rick stepped out with a grin on his face. The love between the two of them shone as they greeted each other with a hug and an intimate kiss. As we walked to the elevator, I trailed behind and watched fondly as they talked quietly, their interlocked hands swinging between them.

When the elevator stopped at the lobby, the doors opened to a smiling Arch. Everyone stepped out and Rick reluctantly released Todd, who exchanged a hearty handshake with Arch. Immediately after releasing their hands, Rick flung his arm around Todd and turned to us. "I'm ready to go, but let me say this now, Cynthia Eleanor Asche, you better let me dance with my husband tonight."

Arch laughed, and his arm encircled my shoulders, mimicking Rick. "We'll likely be fighting over who gets to dance with her. Although, I do want to watch them in action once. I hear it's a sight to see." He laughed and smirked at me. "One more thing… Eleanor?"

I gasped in mock outrage. "It's a family name! Besides, I figured you saw it in my file."

"Besides the initial signing, I've had nothing to do with your case, so I haven't studied your file. I didn't even draft the original document for signing. Meaning Eleanor is a *big* surprise to me." His eyes filled with mirth.

Rick broke out in chuckles. He spared my embarrassment by taking the conversation back to the dancing. "They are impressive. Most likely, we'll end up drinking at a table while they dance. At least until we force them to leave."

I started to argue with him, but bit my tongue—he was right. Grabbing Arch's hand on my shoulder, I pulled him down the hall. "Dance, dance, dance!" I chanted my way to the garage, swaying my hips to my own beat.

As we waited for the others to pull up, I caught Todd staring at my feet. "What?" I asked with a touch of snark.

"I'm excited I got you in heels."

"Heels aren't a totally new thing for me, Todd."

"Not when dancing. You've always worn flats before. This business about needing a more professional image has made you putty in my hands," he said triumphantly.

"I'm glad my stressful lawsuit made your life better." I rolled my eyes at him.

"Me, too, doll face. Me, too."

A horn honked, and I lurched forward, expecting to see one of the guys' SUVs pulling into the parking garage. A high-pitched noise emanated from my mouth I didn't even realize I could make. It was a sound of delight, followed by a similar sound from Todd. Arch's grin answered me, but I asked anyway. "Is this for us?"

When Arch nodded the affirmative, Todd and I ran over to the stretch hummer pulling in. Rick and Arch chuckled behind us.

A chauffeur in a tuxedo bowed slightly as he opened the door for us. I dove in as gracefully as I could. My excitement bubbled over even more when I spied the occupants of the limo. Gray and Wes sat inside. "My gosh, you're already here! I'm as happy as a pig in mud!"

Wes threw his head back and laughed. "I haven't heard that expression since I left Atlanta!"

"My grandmother used to say it."

"She repeats her grandmother's sayings when she gets excited and forgets to filter her mouth." Todd and Rick settled in beside the bar and prepared champagne to hand around. "It's cute the first four thousand times one slips out, but it gets old."

"It doesn't happen often!" I said, indignant. My grandmother used those old southern expressions so often they became a part of my vocabulary for years. She passed away when I was eleven, but the expressions remained. By the time I entered high school, Mitch and Michelle told me repeatedly it was weird, so I stopped. I only used them around Todd.

I accepted a glass of champagne and sat opposite Rick and Todd. The handsome trio sat on the bench seat. "And why shouldn't I be excited? It's not every day we get a limo. When was the last time we rented any sort of car?"

Todd sipped his bubbly and winked. "Senior prom. We got a regular limo." He became distracted by Rick tickling his neck. I turned my attention to the lawyers.

"You look amazing." Gray lifted his glass to me with a smile.

Wes also toasted me. "He's not lying. You're phenomenal."

I tried to look down demurely because that was the appropriate response to such compliments, but it was difficult to restrain my joy. For once, it was possible I did look amazing. "Thank you both. You're pretty phenomenal yourselves." The excitement of the night overwhelmed me, and I bounced a bit in my seat. "Where are we going?"

"First, we're going to eat. The second stop, I'm not telling. It's is a surprise. After we leave there, a club." Arch scooted across the limo to speak to the driver, and we were off.

Gray moved seats to be beside me. "Hermosa, I'm excited to be going out with you tonight, even if it's not an official date."

I smiled at his use of the Spanish pet name. "I know I'm overly excited, a bit, but it's been a long time since I've gone out like this. We're going to have a blast!"

"We are. I can't wait to get you in that dress out on the dance floor." He leaned in, voice soft in my ear. "You've never danced the way I'll lead you."

"Geez," I breathed. Goosebumps erupted all over my body. Gray didn't fail to notice my discomfort.

"What did you do to Ellie?" Wes asked, sliding over to sit on the other side of me.

"Nothing she didn't enjoy." He winked and moved to sit beside Arch.

"He's a flirt," Wes commented.

"And you're not?" I asked, a challenge in my voice.

"He's got me beat." He laughed and threw his arm around me.

The brief kiss Gray and I shared sprang into my mind, causing more goose bumps to erupt. "Do you know where we're headed?" I asked in an attempt to change the subject. I'd never attempted puppy dog eyes on anyone but Todd before, but I was still euphoric over finally besting my stepmother. I decided to take a shot, hoping to sway him to tell me.

He stared at my pouting face, unruffled. "I do. And I'm not telling."

That didn't work out. But it didn't diminish my euphoria. I chatted with Wes about our favorite books until we pulled up to a famous high rise in the downtown area. I pretended to be a real celebrity as I slid out of the limo. Unfortunately, the society reporters were camped in the area waiting on the possibility of an actual celebrity appearance, because as soon as I set one heel-clad foot on the ground, flashbulbs blinded me.

My body froze, blocking the view of the other people in the Hummer. I didn't expect to be recognized and hoped they didn't realize who I was—opposite of my normal, casual self. They'd been obsessed with me since the trial started, but I managed to avoid them more often than not.

One of them recognized me, dashing my hopes of anonymity. "Ellie, over here! Smile for us! Who are you wearing?"

"Ellie!" Todd hissed from behind me. "Smile, walk forward, and wave at the cameras. Rick and I will flank you." I stepped forward one step.

Todd and Rick placed hands on the small of my back, moving me forward. I pasted the most convincing smile I could muster on my face while Todd spoke to the press. He told them the designer of my dress, purse, and shoes, and even who made my jewelry. By the time he ran through everything I wore, we made it inside.

"Why didn't you tell them who made my underwear?" I asked with a laugh as I gave them both a side hug. "Thank you for talking for me and for protecting me."

"That's a secret we'll keep between you, me, and Victoria," he said and pulled me further inside the lobby. "Let's go up to the restaurant and meet the guys. The limo driver is driving them around to a service entrance."

I was taken aback. "Why in the world would they go that way?"

"They said even though they were perfectly allowed to be out with you, they'd prefer not have their faces in the society columns if possible. It takes away from their serious image."

"Okay, I can understand that. Hopefully, by the time this trial is done, the press will forget about me and go back to the socialites. Anyway, I got distracted by the press, but I know where we're going. I've always wanted to eat here!"

"We've been trying to get reservations for ages. We were about to ask you to use your last name to get us some," said Rick.

"Why didn't you ask me before? I rarely use my name, might as well throw it around for you two."

I freshened my lipstick on the long ride to the fiftieth floor. My hair still looked amazing. I was sure by the end of the night it wouldn't be perfect, but it would be proof of a night of fun.

We stepped off of the elevator to a gorgeous view of

the rotating restaurant. Even from our vantage point in the entryway, we could see the phenomenal view. The city lit up as twilight fell. I'd lived here all my life and still loved to watch it come alive at night.

Todd gave my last name to the hostess, and she took us to a large table on the edge of the rotunda, closest to the window. We settled in to wait for my sort-of dates. They walked in as the waitress filled our water glasses.

"That didn't take long," I said by way of greeting.

"We caught all green lights going around the building," said Arch. I smiled at him, glad to be back in their company.

We perused the menu and put in our orders. I settled on the calamari. Gray bought a bottle of wine for the table, and by the time we all poured a glass, it was gone. Wes bought the next bottle. Conversation was stilted and awkward, and the guys gulped their wine.

"What's going on, guys? You're acting strangely." They'd never seemed so uncomfortable around me.

"We want to talk to you," said Wes.

"Rick, darling," Todd cut in, "why don't we go to the bar and enjoy the view from there for a moment." Rick didn't question, and they excused themselves, leaving me alone to my apparently serious conversation.

"Okay, guys. Let me have it," I said, miserable. They didn't want to be around me anymore, I knew it.

"We're all three beginning to care for you," Arch blurted out. "We've allowed becoming friends with you to grow to something more, which we didn't mean to do."

I didn't understand. He meant they never wanted to flirt with me? Why did they, then?

"You intrigued all three of us. We figured out we all wanted to get to know you and decided we'd like to become friends with you. We agreed to try to keep it platonic, at least until you gave some indication of which one, if any of us, you'd like to date," Gray's voice pleaded with me. He wanted me to understand. "I know I, at least, have failed miserably at the friendship-only thing."

"How do I respond to that? I care about you, too, but I care about *all three* of you. I don't know what to do." Misery flooded my heart. Learning more about each of them was supposed to make it easier to choose, but it was getting harder.

"Don't worry about it for now," Wes urged and grabbed my hand. "We're with you through the trial. Until you've gotten that worry off of your mind, we're your friends who care about you and happen to be attracted to you. We'll figure out the rest when your life isn't in such turmoil."

"We'll worry about it tomorrow," I mulled. "Several tomorrows from now, actually."

"That's the grand plan we've come up with thus far," Arch's said in a dry voice.

"Okay. If my friendship is important to you, and you're willing to wait until I win my case, then I'm in. Your friendships have become important to me, also." One thing I knew for sure was I didn't want to lose them. As hard as I tried, I couldn't ignore the agony of the upcoming choice, but I also couldn't face the three of them walking out of my life. The idea of it made me want to hyperventilate and cry.

Our food began to arrive, carried by waiters dressed to the nines. Todd and Rick returned to the table and soon we dug into the delectable cuisine instead of brooding on the conversation. Todd flashed me a questioning look at one point, and I shook my head. I'd fill him in later. He accepted it and returned to his conversation with Gray.

Dinner passed in a blur of city views and friendly banter. Before I knew it, we headed down to the waiting limo. We decided to exit the restaurant together. "If we're going to be your friends, we aren't going to hide it," said Wes as we walked toward the doors.

I took Gray and Arch's arms as we faced the society reporters. This time, I sent them a triumphant smile, instead of forced. I knew my stepmother would see the pictures of me with what she assumed were my lawyers on the front society page in the morning. And she couldn't do a single thing about it.

CHAPTER TWELVE

To my surprise, the limo pulled up to a ballroom dance studio. The guys never ran the evening plans by Todd and didn't know we were practically professional dancers.

I pulled Todd and Rick aside as we walked in. "I guess when I told them we were impressive on the dance floor, they assumed I meant we could bump and grind."

Todd snickered. "Don't tell them what we can do. Start the lesson, then when I cut in on you with them, we'll show them how it's done."

"How long has it been since you two ballroom danced? It's not like riding a bike," said Rick.

"It's exactly like riding a bike, darling. You don't forget." Todd brushed his lips to Rick's to ease the sting of contradiction.

Rick rolled his eyes, but wasn't mad. "Let's get this over with. At the club, you're mine for the first hour,

Todd."

"Absolutely. Let's go."

The instructor paired me with Arch. Gray and Wes awkwardly took each other's hands. The instructor placed their arms appropriately. They both kept trying to lead, bumbling and stumbling over each other. Laughing at the two of them kept my focus off of my debonair partner, to his disappointment.

I pulled it together and played the part of the dutiful student. Todd whispered to Rick as we passed them, "Not like that, my love. I always lead."

Rick replied, "Don't I know it." I stifled a giggle.

We were shown how to hold our hands and the basic box step. We walked through it several times. Once our simple steps satisfied the instructor, a waltz floated over the PA system, and we struck off on our own, boxing our way around the room. "I told Ms. Callie, the instructor, that this was only one lesson for novelty. She isn't trying to lay a foundation for learning," Arch whispered in my ear. "She's making sure we have fun."

"This is the best. And it's about to get better," I said slyly. A confused expression crossed Arch's face as Todd tapped him on the shoulder.

Todd affected a deep tone of voice. "May I cut in?"

Arch turned to me for an answer. I nodded eagerly, and he stepped aside.

"Shall we?" asked Todd.

"Absolutely!" I responded, delighted.

I arched my back and threw my arms out gracefully.

Head tilted, body frozen, I waited for Todd to walk around me and put his right hand under my left shoulder blade to lead me around the room. The familiarity of our holds took me back to our teenage years when we danced every weekend. I closed my eyes and pictured my dad in the audience cheering us on. Serenity flowed over me, and I felt like I was home.

Once he touched my back, he slid his left hand down my right arm and took my hand. Our abdomens pressed tightly together, my back still arched. Todd started twirling us around the room, slowly at first, counting under his breath to get us in the rhythm. The press of his hand told me which way to go and how to move my feet.

With a low dip, Todd kicked it up a notch. I took a deep breath as he started to twirl me. "One, two-three." We began to fall into a faster rhythm. "One, two-three. One, two-three." My blue skirt twirled around me as he spun me across the room, faster and faster. We were born to dance with one another. Todd's feet mirrored mine, and my hold matched his. The years of hard work paid off as I caught glimpses of three shocked faces and one proud Rick.

As the song ended, I spotted Gray out of the corner of my eye, whispering in Ms. Callie's ear. Todd and I threw out our arms, and he bowed while I curtsied. Applause, whistles, and hoots met our final movements.

Gray walked up and gave me a formal bow, one hand out. "May I have this dance?"

"I suppose I have room for one more on my dance

card," I replied.

He clasped my hands and brought them to our sides as the distinctive sounds of salsa came over the loudspeakers. "Cha cha cha," he whispered in my ear, his breath hot on my neck. The music, thankfully, drowned out my moan as his breath on my skin consumed my emotions.

I didn't need to make myself arch my back with Gray. I craved the press of my pelvis against his as he directed our movements on the dance floor. He pulled away from me with a smirk, absolutely aware of his effect on my libido. If this was what friendship meant to them, I was definitely okay with it.

We started several feet from each other. My body knew the way, and I swayed to the beat of the dance, the music moving my feet automatically, my hips falling into the one-two-cha cha cha like an old friend.

Gray was glorious. He danced well enough to have had lessons. After a few circuits, he took me in his arms and pulled me to and fro, our hips in sync to the music and each other. He swayed and thrust, and my hips moved with his as if attached by a short string. He pulled away; I followed. He advanced; I retreated.

He began to twirl me before moving himself around me. I glued my gaze to his. As a student, you learned to watch your partner's face as you danced. I had no issue staring at Gray, looking away was the difficulty. His fluid body led me all over the room, and his whiskey eyes flamed. His hips moved seductively. I couldn't help imagining what else they could do.

The song ended before I was ready to stop dancing. "I could dance like that forever," he said under his breath, his words meant for me only.

"My thoughts exactly," I breathed.

He pulled back and kissed my knuckles as he bowed. My knees went wobbly. I turned to our audience, but we got no applause. Every awestruck eye in the room glued to us.

"If I didn't know how much training you've had, I'd have sworn you and Gray practiced beforehand." Rick broke the silence.

Arch began a slow clap accompanied by a wolf whistle. Wes turned to the instructor. "I want to learn how to do that."

"Do what? The dance, I can teach. The chemistry, you'll figure out on your own," she replied. She turned to me. "I'm inspired. If you two ever want to help teach one of my advanced classes, let me know. I'd love to have you."

Todd chuffed. "We could've cha-chaed like that, too," he whined.

"Of course you could, my love. When we get to the club you can make some chemistry with me, and we'll show these amateurs how it's done." Rick placated him, bringing a smile to his face.

We thanked the lovely Ms. Callie profusely. On the way out, I spotted Gray taking some bills out of his wallet. He murmured a few words to her and attempted to hand her the money. I stopped to wait for him. "I couldn't accept this," she protested.

"I insist. I had the time of my life tonight. You deserve it." He turned and joined me, taking my elbow. "Let's go party."

"Why the big tip?" I had fun, too, but I was sure Arch already paid for her time and tipped when he organized the night.

"I'd pay three times over to dance with you again and feel the desire in your body as you move your hips with mine." Gray gazed deep into my eyes, and the same desire reflected at me.

Friends, you're friends right now, I repeated to myself. *Yeah, that's totally what this is,* I answered myself. *Friends.* I sighed. It didn't matter if we'd decided to declare ourselves friends, enemies, or fairy pirate princesses. We were *not* acting like friends in any way, shape, or form.

"Umm. Wow," I whispered. Words as meaningful as his wouldn't come to my mind. My tongue weighed two tons. "Let's go," I got out. As many romance novels as I'd read in my life, I expected myself to come up with more suave replies.

Gray chuckled as he walked me out to the waiting limo. I slid in and stayed on the bench seat beside Wes. Gray sat beside me.

"You want to learn how to ballroom dance, huh?" I asked Wes.

He nodded the affirmative and grinned at me. "If I get to dance with you, like *that,* the answer is hell yes."

"Let me teach you. There can be a lot of fun in the teaching." The words blurted out of my mouth before I could reel them in. A blush made its way over my cheeks, even as I was suddenly emboldened. I decided to go whole hog and followed my statement with a suggestive waggle of my eyebrows at him.

"I look forward to being an obedient student." His voice was deep, serious, *sexy*. He was laying it on thick. I couldn't bring myself to mind.

Gray leaned over me. "I could teach you, too, Wesssssley." He drew out Wes's name flirtatiously and batted his eyelashes.

"Sit back, you nut. I don't want your ugly mug teaching me."

Gray clasped his chest. "I'm wounded."

I intervened before the testosterone got too ridiculous in the limo. "I'm the only dance instructor you three need. Calm yourselves."

Arch mock saluted from across the limo. "Yes, ma'am!"

We pulled up in front of a black building with a long line of people in various states of fancy dress. A man in a dark suit exited the building and opened the limo door for us. "Asche, party of six?"

"That's us," replied Arch. He handed the man an envelope pulled from a pocket inside his jacket. "Is our table ready?" He leaned over to whisper in my ear. "Your name is handy for making reservations. I hope you don't mind." I winked to let him know it was okay.

"Yes, sir. Please follow me."

I schooled my features for the paparazzi, but inside, I was giddy. I exited the limo as gracefully as I could and allowed Wes and Gray to take my arms and escort me into the club. Arch followed behind me like an ultra-sexy body guard, and Todd and Rick brought up the rear, arm-in-arm. I heard a few murmurs from the crowd, wondering who I was. From the flashbulbs, I knew reporters hid nearby. What a sight I'd be in the papers. I didn't act trashy, and I'd done nothing scandalous, besides act like a normal twenty-one year old for once. I hoped it would bring good press to the company to show me more visible in society.

Once inside the club, the manager walked us to a roped-off alcove marked *VIP*. Even after we entered the relative privacy of the VIP section, the booming club made conversation impossible. Instead of trying to communicate with some weird, inaccurate sign language, I grabbed Arch and Gray's hands and pulled them to the dance floor, motioning Wes to come with us. We spent the next hour dancing—Gray and I danced, anyway. Wes and Arch flailed about with abandon. I would've been embarrassed for them if they weren't so happy in their oblivion.

When our thirst overpowered our desire to dance, we waved at Todd and Rick, dancing nearby, and headed for the table. Once the server delivered our drinks, I motioned for the bouncer guarding our section to close the velvet curtains. The privacy panels provided a break from the volume of the music.

"Now that we are... friends," I stumbled a bit over the word friends. "I wanted to ask a favor from you three." I took a big swig of my potent, pink drink to give me backbone.

"Anything for you. Ask," said Arch.

"The Asche Publishing Christmas party is a week from tonight. I'd like it if you'd go with me."

"All of us?" Wes's eyes widened. He smiled like I handed him a gift.

"You said there's no reason to make decisions now. And we're all friends, right?" I looked to the three of them to reassure me.

"Right," replied Arch.

Gray leaned in and touched my shoulder. "We *are* all friends, and we'd love to go with you to the Christmas party."

"Great! It's a date. A not-date. A nate."

They laughed at my silliness. "How many of those have you had?" Arch pointed to my pink drink.

"One before dancing and this one. I'm pretty sure I burned the first one off on the dance floor." I laughed and downed the rest of the sweet drink.

We chatted about what to wear for the company party, and our upcoming plans for the week as I drank one more yummy cocktail. Then I jumped up. "I came here to dance. Here I go."

Time passed in a blur. I had no idea how long I danced, except, true to his prediction, soon Todd and I danced alone in the middle of a crush of bodies. We weren't your typical bump and grind dancers, though. We alternated between swing, tango, jive, salsa, and some intricate freestyle. We stopped to take quick shots of high-end liquors brought to the dancers by the servers trying to pad the bills with expensive drinks.

Eventually, we headed to the table for a short respite, and four stern faces greeted us. "It's time to go." Rick had his 'I have to talk like a dad or they'll ignore me' voice on.

Todd rolled his eyes. "It's not even late."

Arch checked his phone. "Try again Drunky Dancer. It's midnight."

"Since when is midnight late?" I snarked.

"Since I have to be at the office at nine tomorrow morning." Rick handed Todd the rest of his drink. "Finish your drink, and let's head out." He leaned close to Todd's ear and whispered something.

Todd grinned, threw the rest of his whiskey back and downed it. "I'm ready to go!" He and Rick led the way out of the club to the waiting limo.

I was less willing to leave and kept trying to pull Gray out for one more dance. "C'mon," I shouted in his ear. "We can take a cab! Dance with me!"

He shouted in my ear, but the music drowned his voice. "What?" I asked, tugging on his shirt.

He tried one more time to get me to understand. When I shrugged my shoulders and tried to pull him again, he took matters into his own hands. He bent over, picked me up at the waist, and slung me over his shoulder. I screamed at him to put me down, but of course, he couldn't hear me. I eventually gave up my protests and enjoyed the sexy ride. He put me down before we walked out the door to keep me from being scandalized in the press. I was grateful, but also, disappointed to lose my upside down view of his rump.

The ride home was a bit of a blur. Even with all the dancing I'd done, I still had a hefty buzz. Once upstairs, I was aware enough to dig my keys out of my handbag and even managed to wash off my severely damaged makeup after Arch kissed my cheek and left me to my own devices in my apartment. Before he turned to his place, though, I watched him standing outside my door until he heard the distinctive click of my deadbolt. I set my alarm, downed a huge glass of water to ward off a hangover, and collapsed on the bed, asleep before I could count the first sheep. I didn't even notice Satan jump up on the bed and curl up beside me.

The weekend passed in a whirl of shopping fun. Wes tagged along, saying he used to go thrift store shopping with his mom and sister, and it made him nostalgic. We found sixteen prom dresses and a plethora of cocktail-style dresses. Todd said cocktail was *the* current style. I took his word for it. Poor Wes, bored, held dresses and bags like a champ.

Sunday, we shopped for the Christmas party. Todd and Rick also had an invitation; after all, they were family. We split our shopping time between the men's and women's departments since we needed to find both Rick and Todd a new tux.

Todd must've swished a magic, dress-making wand, because *the* dress appeared in front of me. "Get over here!" I whisper-yelled as I stood in awe. The moment was definitely a bride choosing the perfect wedding gown type of moment.

Todd sidled up beside me, hand over his mouth. "It's perfect. It'll show off your curves, but give you perfect lines. I can't believe it. We found the perfect dress, and it's not even lunchtime. We'll have all afternoon to clean out your closet."

That's what we did. Perfect shoes already sat in my closet, unworn, saving us from shoe shopping. We played in my closet, organizing and sorting, until Rick came home from work. We filled my car to the brim with a cornucopia of clothes to donate.

Monday, we took the dresses to their new homes. It made me happy to send all the unused clothes to people that would get good use out of them.

I received a call from my building manager Monday afternoon while we delivered dresses. The security company figured out who supplied my stepmother with the codes. It was our beloved doorman. He'd already been fired, but with my blessing, they didn't press charges. I was crushed to find out it was someone I cared about. The building super said the doorman had gone through a rough financial time recently. My stepmother probably paid him handsomely for the codes.

To my surprise, Wes turned up Monday evening. "There is something I need to give you," he said.

"Okay, sure! Come in." My heart soared with his sudden appearance.

He didn't give me time to turn and face him before he spun me around and pressed me up against the wall. He trapped me between the wall and his body, and I'd never been so happy to be caught in my life. "I owe you a kiss, friendship be damned." His voice was husky, laced with desire.

His lips crashed into mine, passion inflamed. His hands traveled my body, stopping short of anywhere we weren't ready to go.

My hands drifted to his shaggy blond hair. I traced my fingers behind his ears and to the back of his neck, leaving chills in their wake.

His hands landed on my hips, and with a bit of a crouch, he picked me up by my thighs and carried me over to the couch.

We spent the rest of the evening talking about our futures, desires, and dreams. We peppered the conversation with kisses and caresses. I acted like a high school girl getting to know her first crush. He was sweet and romantic, and his caresses left me with an unquenchable thirst. *Definitely, not just friends.*

I spent Tuesday partly obsessing over the kiss and what it meant, and trying to get Todd to cough up the answer to my problem of who to choose. I wanted to passionately kiss all of them. Only, Arch had yet to kiss me. Once I exhausted Todd's patience, I sat and stewed over whether or not I was immoral to want kisses from three different men.

In the end, I decided I didn't care if I'd be sent to the flaming pits of hell; I wanted those kisses and the opportunity to get to know the guys giving them. Normalcy be damned.

I spent Wednesday at a spa with Todd. We were scrubbed, polished, buffed, and steamed before my big night in a beautiful dress.

Thursday, I gave in. "Todd. Are you busy today?" I called him bright and early.

"Not really. I was gonna deep clean the laundry room." He sounded bored.

"Come dye my hair." Silence. "Todd?"

"Are you serious?" he whispered.

"Yes. I'm ready." I'd begun to enjoy the more girly things in life. I didn't even mind doing my makeup every day.

"I'll be up in thirty minutes. We'll go to the beauty supply store." His voice was extra high-pitched in excitement.

I scurried about and managed to be ready, albeit with wet hair, when he arrived.

We forgot about the frequently present society reporters and took my car to the store. Once they recognized my car, one ran for his own vehicle. "Shit," I muttered.

The reporter didn't disappoint. He managed to follow us to the store, and the next morning there were pictures of me with my damp hair. The headline read, "Wet Hair;

Don't Care." The article was surprising. It complimented me for joining in the fresh-faced, makeup-free Hollywood trend; even though, I was wearing makeup. Thank you to Todd's barely there regime.

We spent the day putting highlights and lowlights in my hair. When Todd turned the blow dryer off on my completed 'do, I couldn't stop staring at myself in the mirror. The change was subtle but impactful, like everything else he'd done.

"Kitten, I keep telling you! You're already beautiful. The changes I've always wanted to make are simply enhancements, not true changes." We stared at my new hair in my bathroom mirror.

He touched my cheek. "Your makeup, if done right, makes your skin glow and your eyes pop." He curled a lock of my hair around his finger. "Your hair, when fixed, is more professional and like you care about yourself. And now the color gives your skin a warm tone and makes your hair shinier and sleeker."

I turned and hugged him. "I'm still me. I still feel like me. I'll still wear the comfy clothes more often than not, though." I stared into the mirror. With the blond highlights, and the small changes to my face, I could glimpse my mom gazing back at me.

Todd burst out laughing. "I have no doubt about that. Rome wasn't built in a day."

In time to save my sanity, Friday appeared. The week had been fun and nerve wracking, but it trudged by like a snail trying to win a grasshopper race. Another one of my grandmother's expressions. Per Todd's instructions, I relaxed all day Friday until time for him to beautify me.

"Tell me why again I wasn't supposed to wash it?" I asked after I showered without washing my hair.

"Dirty hair is easier to style," he replied through a mouthful of hairpins.

"You're the boss." If I hadn't fully trusted his beauty advice before, I certainly did after he proved he was right about my hair color.

Todd started with my hair. He pulled out a box of hot rollers we'd never used before. "This will give you a beachy wave. We'll perfect it with the curling iron."

He applied my makeup while the curlers set my hair. My face was pure elegance when he was done. He finished putting the finishing touches on my bronzed eyes when the buzzer rang from the front door. Someone was in the lobby and wanted to come up. The manager hadn't replaced the doorman, so visitors had to use the buzzers to be allowed in the building.

"I guess they fixed the system." Todd left to check who it was and returned a few minutes later with a manicurist. "I figured of all nights, tonight you get a little extra pampering. She's going to do your nails while I finish your hair.

The small, blond woman set up a collapsible table complete with stool in my bathroom. By the time my nails dried, my hair was cascading down my back in fat curls and waves.

Todd began his own primping while I contemplated

my dress. I stepped into it and instantly turned into a svelte princess—not the old-school, ball gown type princess. I embodied the modern-day, high fashion sort of royalty. Although, I wouldn't have minded a glass slipper. I could rock it.

The sleek black dress had a sheer, embroidered back. The cap sleeves made my arms miles long. The skirt was long—long enough my shoes would only show if I used the finger loop to hold the bottom of the skirt up.

I'd be sure to use the finger loop, though, because they begged to be shown off. They were barely there sandals with a heel high enough I wouldn't be able to dance exuberantly in them. Crystals sparkled on the black leather. Every inch sparkled. Red soles gave a pop of color when I moved my feet.

I was ready to be the belle of the ball. I was ready to wow the board and see my stepmother's face when she watched me walk in on the arms of three of the most eligible bachelors in the city. And, I was ready to work toward gaining a little bit of my Happily Ever After.

CHAPTER THIRTEEN

Todd stood back and watched me preen in the mirror. "You've changed since those three came into your life."

"What do you mean?" I asked, watching him through the mirror.

"You're more confident, and it's nothing to do with wearing makeup." He walked up behind me and put his hands on my shoulders. "I think you've begun to see yourself the way you are—the way I see you."

My reflection was a woman I would've never expected to see. "When did I turn into an adult? I don't feel like an adult." Probably when my daddy died. I stared morosely at the mirror.

"They say it sneaks up on us." He put his arms around me from behind. "You're capable of anything you put your mind to. I want you to believe it."

"I'm beginning to learn it. I'm more confident. I feel

prettier, too." I put my hands on his arms. "Thank you for always finding the best in me."

"It's my job as your fairy godmother. Make you pretty and love you to pieces." He pulled away. "Now. I'm going to go get Rick and meet you at the party. I plan on getting him ridiculously drunk and then having my way with him in your stepmother's office."

"Okay, enjoy!" I laughed as he pranced out of my apartment. A few minutes later, my doorbell rang. I flicked on the monitor to find my dates. The bottom dropped out of my stomach, I took a deep breath and opened the door.

Three dazzling smiles greeted me. "Shall we, sweet lady?" asked Arch with a small bow. He gelled his Ivy League cut hair neatly, but something was off about the way they were dressed. I couldn't put my finger on it.

Gray, long hair loose and shining, stepped forward and pulled a bouquet of roses from behind his back. "For you, on our non-date."

Every petal of the multi-colored roses had an ombre effect. "I love them. Come in, and let me put them in water."

I stared at my pitiful collection of vases under my kitchen sink. It consisted of one vase, too small to hold the roses. Like a proper Southerner, I put them in an old mason jar.

I exited the kitchen to find Gray adjusting Wes's bowtie. His hair was brushed back with barely enough product to keep it in line. "I'm nervous," Wes said to Gray.

"Don't be. It'll all work out," Gray replied as he perfected the tie. As I watched them, I realized what was off about their clothing.

"Everyone ready?" I interrupted their exchange, curious about their conversation but too nervous to ask.

Arch stood behind Gray and Wes, cell phone to his ear. He clicked it off and held his hand out to me. "Your chariot awaits. The limo is a traditional stretch this time." He arranged for the sort of vehicle the board would expect me to arrive in.

"I'm disappointed." I put on a convincing sad face.

Their faces fell. "What's wrong?" Gray exclaimed.

"You're all three wearing capes. I figured you'd be flying me to the party!" I tried to keep up the mock disappointment, but I couldn't. Laughter cracked my facade.

"We've been dying for you to notice!" Wes said through his own laughter.

Gray grabbed his cape and flapped it as he ran around the apartment. "You said capes were a turn on! Do we make you want to rush into the bedroom with us?"

I affected my most serious, sultry voice. "If we weren't on a timeline this evening, I'd be stripping you all three down to nothing *but* the capes." *Good one, Ellie. That's real platonic of you.*

They took a moment to compose themselves, mostly from laughter, but I could see them mulling my words over with lust in their eyes.

"Wait! I almost forgot my earrings!" I ran into my

bedroom to get the diamond drop earrings we bought to go with the dress. Knowing my stepmother would be at her best made me want to be at mine. She'd find no fault in my appearance.

When I walked into the living room, all set to leave, Arch waited for me. He reached out and brushed my hair behind my shoulder. One finger stroked the diamonds dangling from my ear. Physically, his touch was light; I could barely feel him. Sensually, it ran throughout my entire body.

I tilted my face up and gazed into his hazel eyes. His ever-present five o'clock shadow was as light as I'd ever noticed it. His eyebrows rose up in a question. *He's asking permission to kiss me.* The chivalrous gesture turned me on. I slid my hands up his arms and linked them behind his neck.

Tilting my head, I leaned forward and brushed my lips against his, feather light. His breath came hot out of his mouth. He smelled like fresh mint. Tentatively, I slid my tongue along his bottom lip. He opened his mouth, and I darted my tongue inside to meet his.

His resolve to let me lead the way broke, and he pulled me against his body. I could feel the intensity of his desire against my lower stomach. Lava spread across my body at every spot it touched his.

By the time he finished kissing me, I was a quivering mess in his arms. He pulled away, chest heaving. "They'll be waiting for us." I wanted to lock the door and let the world be damned, but I closed my eyes and took a deep, steadying breath.

Arch held out his elbow, and I placed my hand in the crook of his arm. I snatched my lint roller from beside the door and ran it over my dress to capture the stray cat hairs already permeating my home before we joined Arch and Gray at the elevator. "Let's do this. It's probably going to get a little bit ugly tonight," I said with a nervous laugh.

Gray turned and stared at my lips. He knew what we'd done. I waited for an outburst, or at least a glare, but he took my hand and walked into the elevator. On the way down, I pulled a mirror out of my purse and repaired the damage Arch did to my hair and makeup.

The ride over to the Asche Publishing headquarters was tense. We all anticipated the worst from my stepfamily. Arch passed out flutes of champagne. "We shouldn't become drunk tonight, but a little bubbly won't hurt."

"My nerves certainly need it," I murmured.

I finished my champagne as we pulled up to my childhood home-away-from-home. An elderly porter in full formal uniform, including tails, opened the limo door. "Good evening Ms. Asche. I trust you're well."

"I'm wonderful, Reg. How's your wife?" I'd known Reginald for most of my life. He took care of the lobby of our publishing house for as long as I could remember. I received a Christmas card from his family a few days before.

"She's excited about Christmas with the family. They'll be spending the entire holiday with us." He beamed at me.

I grabbed Reg's hand and pressed a small envelope into it. I'd prepared dozens of the envelopes and stuffed my small bronze bag with them. "I hope your holiday is wonderful, Reg. We must get in now."

"Of course, Miss Asche. I hope yours is, as well." He squeezed my hand, and I moved out of the way to allow my dates to exit the limo.

Reg walked ahead of me and held the door open. "Give her hell," he whispered as I passed by. I replied with an exaggerated wink.

"I guess the entire company knows about our battle," I murmured to Arch.

"It *has* been in all the papers," he said as he took my arm.

I led the way to the elevators, and we rose to the event area on the seventh floor reserved for functions: large corporate meetings, company parties, and training events.

The enormous conference room was transformed into a semblance of a winter wonderland. It looked like a high school prom threw up.

Every employee in the company was invited, but we rewarded any employee who needed to work the party a substantial bonus and an extra paid floating holiday for the next year.

"Next year I'll be running this joint, and we can decorate a little better," I said out of the corner of my mouth.

Gray laughed. "You need to put Todd on it."

"That's the truth," came Todd's unmistakable voice

from behind us. "Good man. You're already learning to let me take care of things."

Once we greeted one another, we moved as one unit toward the center of the room. I spied my stepsister across the room and strategically placed myself behind Arch and Gray. Wes stood with me. "Now what?"

"Now, I need to go find members of the board and schmooze a little. Would any of you like to join me?"

Arch responded first. We left Gray and Wes with Todd and Rick at our shared table. I approached the acting CEO first. "Scott, it's nice to see you this evening. Where's your lovely wife?" I asked.

"She's a bit under the weather tonight." He smiled and shook my hand with a limp grip.

"This is my friend, Arch Beaumont. Arch, this is the interim CEO of Asche, Scott Allen."

The two men shook hands. "What do you do, Arch?" Scott affected a jovial tone, which I knew to be a lie. The man was incapable of anything but a foul expression on his face.

"I work in a law office," he replied evasively.

"I see." Scott sounded disinterested. He probably expected Arch to respond with some impressive career—which, ironically, he did have—but Arch wouldn't give him any information about himself.

Scott cleared his throat importantly. "Ellie, how's the mess with your mother going? Have either of you come to your senses yet?"

I raised one eyebrow, the only sign of irritation I'd

give him. "My ex-*step*mother and I are in the middle of a complicated legal battle, as I know you're aware. I'm sorry, but I'm not at liberty to discuss it here."

"I understand, of course." He peered around the room, searching for a reason to make his exit. "I must excuse myself, I see…" He trailed off as he scurried away.

Arch's hazel eyes were bewildered. "What's his problem?"

"I'm certain he's the one trying to turn the board against me." If looks could kill, Scott would've had a dagger in his back.

"Do you think Raquel is buying him off?"

I shrugged my shoulders. "That's my guess. I hope so, at least. If she is, there will be a trail. That's one thing my lawyers are looking into."

"Time is beginning to run short. Your next meeting with the judge is in a few weeks isn't it?" I didn't see any more board members yet. I led Arch toward our table.

"Yes." I sighed and studied Arch's face. His hazel eyes turned green under the twinkling Christmas lights. "I wish I could at least discuss the case with you."

"Have faith. Something will turn up. No judge in their right mind will give this place to her." He gave my hand a reassuring squeeze. "Let's focus on fun tonight. Maybe we can sneak away for a little tour," he said with a roguish wink.

I pushed his shoulder playfully. "You wish."

"He wishes what?" asked Wes.

"None of your business, Wesley Earl Lawson," Arch

chided.

"Wesley *Earl* Lawson?" I couldn't believe my ears. "Your names are Archibald Duke, Gray Baron, and Wesley Earl?"

Three sets of cheeks turned pink. Wes and Gray nodded their heads reluctantly, and Arch replied, "Unfortunately."

I clapped my hands delightedly. "You guys are my little posse of royalty? Like my charming princes or knights in shining armor?" What an excellent secret. I was sort of dating royalty.

"I tried to tell you our parents are strange. When they found out they were all pregnant at the same time, they wanted to put a theme to our names," said Wes.

"We actively try to keep people from discovering that little tidbit," added Gray.

"Delightful. Absolutely delightful. I have to start calling you by your royal names, of course. Come along, Earl. I'll start teaching you to dance. Todd and Rick are already out there." I scanned the room again. "I still don't see the rest of the board. Maybe they'll come in while we dance."

"As you wish, my lady," my Earl replied.

I didn't try to teach him anything. We stood close to one another and shuffled side to side like a couple of kids at their high school prom. It gave us a chance to talk. "I want to know more about your families. We've talked about everything under the sun but them." Wes's back stiffened, and I pulled my head away from his chest.

"What's wrong?"

"Ellie, our families are a sensitive topic for us. We don't like talking about them. I promise, though, we will, soon." My curiosity burned, but I let the matter rest. I didn't want to make him uncomfortable.

"What do you dream of, Ellie? What'd make you happy in life?"

I sighed and contemplated all the opportunities given to me in life. "I want to run this company until I retire. And I want to raise my children here, the way I was raised. I spent more time here than home as a child."

"I have every confidence in you." Wes led me into a little spin and pulled me closer.

"She doesn't deserve this company. It was built by my family, and one of us should always be at the helm."

"What'll you do when you win?" His surety of the trial outcome made me chuckle.

"First, I want to finish college. I want to appoint my own interim CEO to manage things in my absence." I put my head on Wes's chest. "There are women here that have been shunted to the side since my father died. Long term, dedicated employees who could take this place and run with it. Dad had specific goals, you know?"

"Did he leave any of them in writing?"

"I couldn't find them. I searched high and low for weeks after he died, but she must've found and destroyed them." Another reason to hate the horrid woman.

"What was his vision?" The song ended and a quicker tempo started up. Wes led me off the dance floor and toward the bar. I nodded a hello to the young, lanky bartender. "You're Thomas Elmore's son aren't you? Tom from accounting?"

"Yes ma'am. I'm working my way through college." He gave me a wavering smile.

I opened my handbag and slipped him two of the envelopes. "Merry Christmas. If you spot your dad around, tell him to say hi."

"Yes, ma'am. Thank you!" He tucked the envelopes into his black apron.

Wes and I moved off to the side of the bar, giving us relative privacy.

"Dad wanted to promote more women. His dream was to see me lead a company of strong women. He talked about the glass ceiling a lot. By the time he retired, I'd be ready to take over, and he hoped to have a board full of women to advise me."

"It's an admirable goal. Many men his age have the opposite outlook."

"He was a wonderful man. I miss him dearly." My gaze covered the filling room, seeking out the women my father had been grooming to promote, but instead, I landed on the table where Arch and Gray waited for us. They were being harangued by my stepsister.

"We need to go save them," I said, pointing to the table.

"Who's that?"

"My stepsister. Miss Popularity herself." The pending confrontation gave me an instant headache. I touched my nauseous stomach, dreading the coming cattiness.

A warm hand touched the small of my back. "Don't sweat it. You've got us, and if need be, we'll find Todd. You're not here alone."

Such a support system was a novel experience. For most of my life, it was only Dad and Todd on my team.

I marched my way over to confront Michelle. She wore a backless pink dress with an awful bow on the butt. Her bony back faced me as she leaned across the table.

As I walked up, I caught the tail end of her words. "...gives you any trouble, you tell them to find Michelle. I'm important around here. If I vouch for you, they won't say a word."

I started to tap her on the shoulder, but stopped myself. Pretty sure she was trying to flirt; I wanted to listen to the rest of her conversation. "My mother is in the process of taking this place over. They won't say no to me. I don't know why you won't tell me who you're with, but I promise nobody will bother you." Arch and Gray pointedly ignored her. They were so focused on not paying her any attention they didn't even notice me walk up.

"Michelle, they're here with me," I announced.

She whirled around, revealing the front of the dress—worse than the back. Arch and Gray swung their heads around to face me, relief evident in their expressions.

"Cynthia." Michelle's voice dripped ice.

"You know I don't go by my first name, Michelle." *Why do you bother trying to correct her?*

She rolled her heavily made up eyes. Her makeup

looked like it was applied by a circus clown's makeup artist. "Whatever."

"Why are you going around telling people you basically run this place? You know it's not true." *And never will be, bitch.*

"You won't win this case. You don't have a leg to stand on. It's inevitable. My mother will be in charge. Then, you'll pay for what you did to Mitch."

I bit down on my tongue before I flew off the handle. Wes pushed up close behind me and whispered in my ear. "Stop talking to her. Everything needs to be done through the lawyers."

"Michelle, if you have anything further to say, you can call my lawyer's office." I stepped back, wordlessly asking her to leave.

She stomped off on heavy pink heels, too clunky for the dress. "Todd would have a field day with her style. Where is he?"

Arch pointed to the dancers. "Still wrapped around Rick."

I watched my friends dance for a moment with frayed nerves, acutely aware of six eyes on me. "Are you okay?" asked Gray.

"She's crazy, you know." Arch stood and took my hand. I stood in a Wes and Arch sandwich, and it comforted me, slightly. I didn't care who watched us. "Anyone that didn't know you would be able to see through her right away. And anyone that does know you wouldn't give her the time of day."

"My brain understands. My heart is another story." Tears welled up in my eyes. "Excuse me, I need the restroom."

With no desire to use the restroom, I headed for my dad's office. I'd had the lock changed after he died. No one could use the space until I could decide what to do with it. I wanted a moment to be near him again.

When I reached his double doors, they were cracked open, light spilling out. Alarm filled my stomach. Nobody had a key but me, and mine was in the purse in my hand. I slowed my steps and approached the office as quietly as I could. Soft noises from within made me freeze. A distinctive moan floated out the crack in the door, then a man said, "Raquel."

My stepmother was inside my father's office with another man! I took two deep breaths, trying to decide what to do. If I confronted her, there was the possibility no one would believe me.

My phone. I pulled my cell out of my bag. Luckily, I'd put it on silent before the party. Launching the camera, I double checked the flash was off and hit record.

Surreptitiously, I glanced around to check nobody was nearby to witness me get down on my knees and slip the phone inside the door. I could see the screen and could tell I definitely filmed something, but the angle was bad, and I couldn't make out anything specific. I let it record. Truth be told, I had no desire to watch what happened in the room, but I knew I needed to get the proof. It was my big break.

Several minutes later, my legs burned, and my arm felt like it was going to fall off from holding the phone out. Laughter floated up the hallway behind me. I pulled the phone out and turned off the camera. I waited in the office beside my dad's until the giggling couple passed by.

I peered into the hallway. Dad's office door was shut. The lovebirds noticed the passersby and pushed the door closed. I ran on tiptoe toward the party as fast as I could in the heels, slowing to a normal pace when I passed someone in the hallways.

Thankfully, Rick and Todd sat at the table when I arrived. I tugged on the first arm I came to—Wes's. "Come with me, please. Todd, Rick, do you know where the cafeteria is?"

They both nodded, giving me curious stares. "Where have you been?" Todd hissed at me.

"In a minute," I whispered. "Discreetly bring Arch and Gray down there. It should be empty now; all of this was catered externally. Don't come together, split up and play it nonchalant." My head spun with the information I'd gathered.

I gave a winning smile, congratulating myself on my acting skills, and took Wes by the hand. "I'll show you to the restrooms," I said for the benefit of anyone standing nearby.

As soon as we left the room, we hurried to the elevators. "We need to get out of sight," I said.

"Why?" Wes watched me like I was a firework about to explode.

"Not here. Act normal." My eyes darted around. It was hard for me to follow my own advice and act normal as keyed up as I was about the video in my phone.

Several people exited the elevator to join the party. I introduced Wes to a few people I'd known all my life. I handed out more envelopes and asked about families. Externally, I was a calm, professional cucumber. Inside, I was a pickle, screaming with anticipation.

We entered the empty elevator and headed for the service level. I pulled Wes to me for a hug. "The elevators are monitored, and I think they have microphones. Someone tried to steal a highly anticipated sequel one time, and we upped security," I began to whisper. "If anyone catches us down there, we'll pretend we were seeking out some privacy."

"What's going on?" Wes asked. "I'm worried."

I simply shook my head. I needed them all to watch the video I took and tell me if my hopes were up for nothing or if I had won my case. I still wasn't sure what I recorded. If it was Scott and my stepmother having sex, it would at least sway my case.

Once we were safely in the cafeteria, I collapsed into a chair, relieved. We made it.

"Now, will you tell me what the hell is going on?" He wore his blond hair slicked back, and it was disheveled. He'd been running his fingers through it, and I hadn't even noticed. My evasive behavior upset him.

"I'm sorry, Wes, but I have no idea where all the cameras and microphones are. As soon as everyone shows up, we're going to go into the bathroom across the hall. I know there are no surveillance devices in there."

Wes gave me a look saying clearly, I'd spoken another language. "I'm being far too cautious and overly dramatic, but this is my future on the line. I need to be sure." I couldn't risk Raquel finding out I shot the video before I was ready for her to know.

The arrival of Todd and Arch saved me from any further explanations. I jumped out of the chair as they entered. "Rick and Gray should be right behind us. What the *hell* is going on?" Arch demanded.

"Not yet. Wait until they get here." Three faces stared at me like I'd grown horns. Pacing seemed the thing to do while we waited. Rick and Gray burst in moments later, causing me to jump and scream.

Gray was furious. "What's wrong with you? Are you hurt? Did someone hurt you while you were gone?" He grabbed my hands and began to check me over.

"No! I'm not hurt. Follow me, and I'll explain everything." Peeping out of the cafeteria, I peered up and down the hall. I couldn't see anybody, and I was pretty sure the stretch of hall didn't have cameras. If security was watching the cafeteria, they wouldn't know where we'd gone, giving us enough time to get the explanations out of the way. There was no way I could've waited until we got home, which would've been the smartest thing to do.

When the coast was clear, I bolted across the hall to the bathroom. Holding the door open, I gestured for them to all follow. Wes murmured something to them, which spurred them along. I fought laughter as they all looked both ways to make sure nobody spotted them.

The comedy of the situation hit me hard. We played secret agent, running around a large company like children. It would've been fun if I wasn't apprehensive about what was on my phone.

The bathroom was basic—nothing like the swanky bathrooms where we entertained clients. I rolled my neck and took a deep breath. "Okay. I need advice."

Arch shook his head and seemed to be trying hard not to roll his eyes at my dramatics. "Start at the beginning, please."

"I'm not sure how much you're allowed to know, given you're practicing lawyers, and you're the partners of my lawyer. If I get into information you shouldn't know, tell me immediately."

"We're allowed to know information. We're not allowed to give advice." Wes reassured me they'd help in any way they could, ethically.

"I got overwhelmed after speaking to Michelle," I began.

"You should've called me. I would've taken care of that bitch." Todd was pissed.

"Todd! Focus." Rick reined him in.

"Thanks, Rick. I wanted to be near my dad for a while. I went to his office on the top floor, but someone was in there. I figured out it was Raquel with a man. I'm almost positive I know who the man was, but there's no way in hell I'm watching this video. I need someone else to watch it and tell me if I shot a video of Raquel having sex with Scott Allen, the interim CEO of Asche Publishing."

Todd and Rick gasped in unison. "If that's what you found, then this case is over, pumpkin!" said Todd.

I looked at Arch, Gray, and Wes. They all had huge smiles on their faces. "I know you three can't comment, but I'll take your smiles as this is a good thing for my case."

Arch shrugged. "You'd have to ask your lawyer." He continued to smile though.

"I need someone else to watch it. I can't stand to see it." I handed my phone to Todd.

"Yuck," he said, but he tapped away at the screen, pulling up my videos. He hit play, and all five guys crowded around the phone in his hand.

The microphone on the cell picked up more volume than I'd been able to hear in person. When I realized there was more to their tryst than canoodling, I crowded in with them.

The screen showed them doing some heavy petting and kissing, but thankfully all clothes remained on. Their words excited me. "Scott, I've upheld my end of the bargain. I need you to deliver the board to me. Unless we get more of them on our side, our plan will never work."

"Are you sure it'll work?" The slimy CEO pulled away from Raquel's neck, giving the camera a crisp view of both of their faces.

"How many times do I need to explain this?" Raquel pushed Scott to arm's length. "We win the lawsuit. I take over as CEO. We prep the company to sell, then the night before the news breaks, we sell our stocks. All of my stocks are already in a fake name. We need to sell yours to the same fake name before I get control of the company. Then the sales won't be traced to us. I know a guy that can do it entirely under the radar."

"You're exciting when you're being devious." He began to lift her dress, and I jumped and turned away. Mercifully, the video cut off before anyone was subjected to my naked stepmother.

Todd said what everyone thought. "This is it, Ell. Show this to the judge, and it's all over."

"I wondered though... Couldn't I show it to Raquel and basically blackmail her into dropping the suit? Wouldn't it be faster and easier?" My three non-lawyers gave me serious, unhappy looks.

"That's too generous. They need to pay for what they tried to do," replied Todd.

I glanced at my silent judges, and they smiled again. "You three are kinda creepy." They chuckled but continued their silent treatment.

"I do think you'd be allowed to answer this," I began. "When this is turned over to my lawyer, will she go to jail?"

"Yes," said Arch. "Most likely."

Gray pushed forward and pulled me into a hug. "Relax, gorgeous. It's become a night to celebrate. Before we go upstairs and dance our pants off, perhaps you have something you want to e-mail so it's saved on more than one server? In case something happened to your phone."

"Oh!" I gasped. "Great idea." I grabbed my phone from Todd and e-mailed the video to Todd, Rick, and myself. That way if something *did* happen, it would be saved on three different servers.

"Let's go celebrate!" I chirped.

CHAPTER FOURTEEN

Champagne and laughter filled my evening. I passed out the rest of my envelopes and pictured my father's smile every time I tucked one into someone's hand. I was called up to the small stage to give a speech—luckily, before drinking too much champagne.

"Good evening, all. I had no idea I'd be asked to give a speech tonight. Forgive me for doing this off the cuff." I took a sip of my drink and clutched the podium nervously. "I've known many of you since I was a small child, running around these offices." There were a few faces in the crowd I'd known since birth. I pointed to a few of them. "Several of you were with my family before we even bought this building. Remember the tiny office across town?" Heads nodded along with me, and a number of people laughed.

"My family built this company, but they didn't do it

alone. Each one of you had a hand—some of you a large hand—in our success. I don't know how to thank you for it, but I'll find a way. I'm incredibly proud of what this company has become and of the people we work with." I raised my glass to the room. "May your holidays be wonderful. I hope Santa is good to you all this year." I sipped my champagne, and the room sipped theirs before breaking into applause.

I stepped down from the podium to many handshakes, hugs, and condolences. It was heartening to hear many people whispering encouragement—they wanted me to win the lawsuit. Barely stopping myself from shouting my news, I smiled and thanked them.

The party began winding down at ten. I'd been circling the room with one or another of my friends all evening. I gestured to all of them to join me, and we began working our way out of the room. Raquel had the same idea. We met up with her outside the doorway. I held out my hand. "After you." I smiled my sincerest, sweetest smile. "I hope you have a wonderful evening, Raquel." She narrowed her eyes at me in suspicion, but never said a word. I hoped she enjoyed herself. It would be her last fun night for many years to come.

She stopped and turned to me. Her face was nearly green, and she looked like she'd swallowed a lemon. "Ellie," she said softly.

I glared at her, disgusted. "What?" I fought to keep the smile off my face.

Her eyes darted around us and lingered on my friends.

"Can I ask you something privately?" she whispered.

"No." No quarter for that bitch.

"It's Mitch. He told me what happened at your apartment, and I... he needs help." I'd never seen her look so vulnerable.

"Of course he needs help, Raquel. He's sick." I couldn't find sympathy.

"He won't get any help in jail. You have to know that." Her expression pleaded, desperate. I nodded my head. "If I forcibly check him into a psychiatric facility he can't voluntarily check himself out of, would you drop the charges?" She grabbed my arm. "Please."

I studied her, broken down and desperate, and considered what I had on my phone. She'd be in jail soon enough. There was no help available for her. But Mitch, he seemed to be out of his mind. "If my lawyers are satisfied he can't check himself out and he's in a good place, I'll drop the charges."

Her shoulders slumped in relief. "Thank you, Ellie. I don't want my son to spend years in jail over something you did to him when you were teenagers."

My sympathy evaporated and my heart turned to ice. I plastered a sunny smile on my face. "Goodnight, Raquel." I wouldn't ever have to hear her voice again. Soon.

The ride home was quiet until we neared the building. "Ellie," Arch said. "Are you tired? Could we come over? We'd like to talk to you." Todd chuckled softly and winked at me.

"I'm wired. I'd love your company." What could they

possibly want to talk about? Maybe they'd decided for me. One of them wanted to go further, and the other two didn't. Maybe none of them did.

"Great," replied Gray as we pulled into the garage. Wes tipped the driver and sent him on his way. Their cars were parked next to Arch's. "We may crash on your couches tonight."

It was fine with me if they stayed close. I'd begun to crave their companionship, and the last talk with Raquel about Mitch had me unnerved again.

I slipped off my heels when we reached the carpeted interior of the building. The elevator ride to Todd's floor was quick. He hugged me and whispered in my ear. "Get 'em, tiger."

My face flushed bright red as he and Rick headed to their apartment and we continued upstairs. I unlocked my apartment with a nervous stomach, beginning to imagine less savory conversations.

Once inside, I offered drinks. "I don't think we should drink anymore," said Wes. "We've pretty clear heads right now and some serious stuff to talk about."

"Serious?" My nervous stomach started rolling. They'd decided it wasn't worth fooling with me anymore and were going to go their separate ways. What else could it be?

"Yeah. Lots to talk about." Arch sat on the couch. "Come sit." Full of apprehension, I joined him. "We want to tell you about our families." Gray sat beside me, and Wes sat on the coffee table, facing me.

Their families—not at all what I expected. "Okay." I

could handle that. "Why's it a serious conversation? I know a little bit. They live in Atlanta on a farm they run together. The farm has become a popular, lucrative place."

"There's more to it than that," said Wes. "It's a little hard to explain." Wes stared wide-eyed at Gray.

"We don't have traditional parents." Gray's voice hesitated. He was scared to tell me something.

I didn't understand what the big deal was. "Okay. They're not married, or they're gay or something? I'm pretty open minded."

"Not exactly." Arch looked at the others before turning to me, like he drew strength from his friends. "Ellie, our parents are polyamorous."

"Poly...? Like, sister wives?"

"Nothing as dramatic as what you see on TV or read online, but yes. They're in a relationship with more than two people." Gray held his breath after his explanation.

"Okay. Like a triad?"

"My parents are a triad, yes," said Arch patiently. "I have two dads and a mom."

"But, who's your biological dad?" The concept was foreign to me. I'd heard of it before, of course, but I'd never met someone in such an unconventional relationship.

"Now that I'm an adult I know whose sperm made me, but I didn't until I was eighteen. Until I got curious, it never mattered. I was showered in love, which was all that mattered."

"Okay." It was a lot to swallow, but it made sense.

"Gray. You said you have nine brothers and sisters?"

"Yes, Hermosa. I have three moms and one dad." He closed his eyes. He was scared of my reaction.

"That's definitely a new one for me. Did you know who your birth mother was?"

"Yes, but I called them all some version of Mom. They were all my parents, and like Wes and Arch, there was no shortage of love in our home."

"My family is the hardest to swallow, Ellie," said Wes.

"Lay it on me." I took the news pretty stoically. It was definitely a whole new ballgame.

"I have four dads and two moms." His blue eyes were wide and pleading. His face clearly begged me to accept him and not judge him.

"Okay. I'm sure I'll have more questions about how it works, if you're willing to share, but why are you three freaked out?" I understood their apprehension, and why they didn't tell people about their backgrounds. They were scared.

"We've told few people about our families," Arch said.

Wes took a deep breath. "I was in a pretty serious relationship about three years ago. We lived together, and I asked her to marry me. A month before the wedding, I broke down and told her about our parents. It started a rift and eventually broke us up."

"Why in the world would your parents' relationships have anything to do with your relationship with her?" It made no sense. They were in a monogamous relationship, unrelated to his parents. "That would be like blaming someone if their parents got divorced."

"It was pretty messed up." Arch ran his fingers through his short hair. It ended up going in thirteen different directions. He was cute when stressed.

Gray twirled his hair around his fingers. All three of them messed with their hair when upset. "With the exception of Penny, we'd told a few girlfriends along the way, and it ended badly. None of them handled it well. Penny knew all along."

"We learned early to hide it from friends. Eventually, we stopped trying to make close friends outside of the three of us. Our partners at the firm don't even know about our family dynamics." Wes ran his fingers through his hair as well, making it frizz a little.

"I know you lived in the south, but it seems like people wouldn't hold your parents' decisions against you." I hoped we'd progressed beyond that level of judgment.

"It wasn't the south." Wes's voice was dejected. "Back then, if we took a vacation and anyone figured out what sort of relationship our parents were in, they gave dirty looks, said rude things under their breath, and sometimes got a little physical. It happened wherever we went."

My heart hurt for them. They were children and had to learn how cruel the world could be. "I'm sorry you experienced the worst in people so early in life."

"Yeah, well... With all that in mind, how do you feel about dating us?" Arch's voice was so soft I could barely hear him.

"It doesn't change anything. If and who I date, it won't matter what sort of relationship your parents are in." I contemplated the three men who turned my life upside down. They helped me find confidence in myself and believe I could run a multi-million dollar company. I felt beautiful, inside and out, every time I was around them.

They couldn't have appeared more different, yet they were brothers, in every sense of the word except biological. I studied Arch with his mussed hair, hazel eyes, and overprotective nature. He was miserable behind his pronounced five o'clock shadow. He watched me stare at him. His eyes implored me, but I didn't know the question. I wouldn't reject them, not as a whole, but at some point, I'd be forced to choose.

I moved my gaze to Gray. Romantic, sensual Gray. He held a strand of his long hair in front of his face, studying the ends. He caught me staring at him and met my gaze with a challenge. His light brown eyes, like cognac, were scared, even as his whiskered chin lifted in defiance.

Wes was the last to get my scrutiny. He stared at the floor, his shaggy hair mostly blocking his face as it hung down around him. His shoulders slumped. I was pretty sure he already admitted defeat. He figured I'd reject them based on their parents' decisions.

The idea of the three of them walking out of my apartment and never coming back made my chest ache. Tears sprang to my eyes. "Stop looking sad," I demanded.

Wes's face came up, surprise written all over it. "What do you mean?"

"Our problem isn't me accepting your family. I accept them. They aren't you. Our problem is you all have feelings for me, don't you?" Three nods. "I have feelings for all three of you. What're we supposed to do? I don't think I can choose one of you! And if I did, what would it do to the other two of you?" My heart was torn. I couldn't come up with one thing to elevate one above another and make the decision easier.

"We hoped you'd come to this on your own, but we want you to be in a relationship with us." Arch turned those pleading eyes on me.

I stared at them blankly. "I know. That's what we've been talking about." My mind went a little fuzzy. I tried to understand what they meant, but I couldn't process it.

Gray took my hand and turned it palm up. He traced the lines as he spoke. "Hermosa, *we* want to date you. Us." He pointed to himself, then Arch and Wes. "All of us. Dating you."

Blinking repeatedly, my brain finally connected. Lightning exploded through my eyes, relief flooded my belly. Warmth spread across my heart, and my chest stopped hurting. The stress I carried since I realized I had feelings for all three of them evaporated. I finally understood what people meant when they said a weight lifted off their shoulders.

I realized I hadn't spoken for several long seconds. Their expressions turned to bitter disappointment while I contemplated how amazing it could be to date all three of them. "No! No sadness! This is fantastic!" I threw my arms out, light as a feather. My company would be mine, and my guys would, too!

"Fantastic?" Hope blossomed on Arch's face. Wes gripped the edge of the coffee table. Gray tugged on a chunk of his hair. "You're happy about it?"

"Yes! Oh, sure, there will be issues. Jealousy, timing, families—I mean, where do we go for holidays? Do your families holiday together? Who sleeps where? Ugh, jealousy. But, for now, it doesn't matter." Even though they'd grown up in unconventional families, they'd never been in a relationship like their parents before. There were bound to be speed bumps in the road.

"Logistics like those kind of work themselves out." Wes grinned his breathtaking smile at me, pearly teeth flashing.

"We did learn a thing or two from our parents' mistakes, too," said Arch.

"And I'm sure they'll be able to give us advice," added Gray.

"I don't want to discuss big stuff yet. No kids talk, or marriage talk, or anything like that. We're getting to know each other." The heavy stuff could wait. We were still young. We had time to get to know one another.

"Are we going to do this? You're going to be *our* girlfriend?" Gray practically vibrated with excitement.

"I am. I'd be honored to be your girlfriend." I tried to take in all of them at once. With huge smiles pasted on their faces, they all lunged at me. Soon I had three muscular men piled on me. "Uncle! Uncle! I give!" They hugged, kissed my cheeks, and tickled me into submission. "You win!"

One by one they climbed off the couch, kissing my cheeks as they passed. I wanted to jump up and down, excited about the prospect of our future together. I got to keep all three of the men I'd grown to care for. It could be difficult, but if it continued being as rewarding as the past month had been, it would be worth every second spent together.

EPILOGUE

Ellie stared across the auditorium at her husbands-to-be. They turned their gazes toward her, music filling the air. Her best friend, Todd, stood just before her, ready to walk her down the aisle. "Oh, God, Ell. They look like sin in suits standing up there."

She smiled at her lifelong best friend. "Thank you, Todd."

"For what, duckie?" Todd gave her hand a squeeze.

"For being with me. For being my family, my best friend. My matron of honor." Ellie sniggered. "Man of honor?"

Todd chuckled. "I prefer BrosMaid." He stuck his nose in the air. "BrosMatron? BridesBro. Oh, whatever. You're my family, Ellie. It's you and me against the world. Let's go get you married to your wet dreams." As her oldest friend and chosen family, Todd clasped Ellie's arm and turned to walk her down the aisle.

Thanks to Todd's wit, Ellie forgot her butterflies and stepped into the aisle with laughter in her throat, but her mirth died while she glided toward the men she loved. They watched her advance with predatory gleams in their eyes, a promise of the wedding night to come. She was about to be handed over to the care of her three loves when Todd leaned in. "I've got it. BridesQueen." Ellie held in her laugh but couldn't stop a snort. Arch, Wes, and Gray watched her compose herself, amused, and the seriousness of the moment calmed her emotions—somewhat.

The guests watched their friends marry in scandalized glee. The wedding was in ceremony only, as polygamy was still illegal in the US, but the newlyweds didn't care. They relished the chance to show their love to the world and hoped to help create some normalcy for so-called alternative lifestyles.

One by one, Ellie exchanged vows with Arch, Wes, and Gray. "I promise to keep our family and our interests number one in my life. I promise to love you and hold you in my heart, until the day I die. I promise to sit down with you when we are mad and figure out how to fix whatever the problem is. I promise to honor your wishes and consider them in any major decisions I make. I promise to always stay in contact with you and not make you worry. I promise to bring fire to your life so that we never get bored. I do not promise to obey, because that's just creepy."

The attendants tittered with laughter as Ellie gave

Arch a soft kiss.

Turning to Gray, she continued. She repeated the first part of her vows, promises to each of her husbands, to keep their family first in her heart. She ended with, "I promise to do everything I can to stay out of a hospital, so that you do not have to set foot in one. And I promise to never try to outdo your mama's cooking. I will sing with you and read bad comic books. For all my life, I will be yours."

A strangled sob, or maybe it was laughter, came from the audience, and Gray's biological mother, Rosa, hair streaked with silver, dabbed her eyes. Gray looked at his parents, love and concern written on his face. His three mothers sat with a silver-bearded man. The women clasped hands, and Rosa nodded to Gray so the ceremony could continue.

Ellie gave Gray a soft kiss and faced Wes. After her promises, Ellie concluded her vows with, "My genius surfer dude. I promise to read with you and pick books to publish with you. I promise to work out with you, even though I'll hate every single second of it, but I know how much you want me to be healthy. I promise to cook for you and I look forward to many meals prepared by you." After giving Wes a kiss, Ellie stood back and braced herself to fight tears while her men spoke their vows to her.

Arch spoke next. "Ellie, we wrote our vows together. We started to do them separately but when we compared notes we realized we were stepping on each other's toes."

Ellie's heart swelled. "I think that's appropriate."

Wes continued, "Cynthia Eleanor Asche, we promise, first and foremost, to be continuously aware of our jealousy levels. We promise to talk to you and each other if we begin to feel the little green monster rear up."

"The day you walked into our lives was the day the world settled into place for all of us," said Gray. "We didn't know it right away, but you were the missing puzzle piece. We won't be so corny as to say you completed us, but you certainly brought a funny, quirky dynamic personality into our lives that none of us ever want to be without."

"We want to grow old with you. We want to spoil grandbabies and argue over the best way to irritate our kids," said Wes.

Arch chuckled before speaking his part. "We want to become so familiar with you that you always finish our…" He paused and looked at Ellie with raised eyebrows. "Always finish our…"

Ellie gave them a bewildered stare.

"Sentences, Ellie. We want to be close enough that you always finish our sentences."

The audience burst into laughter, and Ellie's eyes danced with mirth.

"We promise to be your family and to share our large family with you." Wes spoke to Todd over Ellie's shoulder. "And to be family to Todd and Rick, no matter what the years may bring."

"We promise to get up and get the remote from across

the room, so that you can change the channel to make us watch shows we really don't even kind of want to watch, even if we are not the ones who left the remote all the way across the room," Gray said through chuckles.

Arch, standing in the middle, stepped forward. "We can't wait to take the next step in our lives together. We can wait to be your husbands." He kissed Ellie on the cheek and pulled back.

Wes, on Ellie's right, slid forward and took Ellie's hand. "We can't wait to have babies. Or adopt, or get dogs, or whatever we might decide, as long as it's with you." He kissed Ellie on her other cheek and withdrew.

Gray stepped close to Ellie and, dropping his voice, spoke words only she, her husbands-to-be, and Todd could hear. The officiate had moved to the side for the vows to be spoken and was just out of earshot. "We promise to always think of you first in the bedroom. You will never go unsatisfied as long as any of the three of us draws breath in our lungs. And tonight especially, *Hermosa*, you *will* be satisfied." He placed his hands on her cheeks and drew his lips to her forehead. With his lips still grazing her skin, he whispered, "Over, and over, and over."

As Ellie's knees went weak and goose bumps erupted over her body, Todd began to fan himself. "Dear Jesus, *Lord,* get on with this wedding before I keel over dead!" he exclaimed.

Laughter filled the room once again. Thanks to Todd's inability to control the volume of his voice, everyone got the gist of what Gray had whispered to Ellie. He shot the crowd a devilish grin, and the officiate completed the ceremony.

"As I understand it, the grooms played rock, paper, scissors to determine in what order they would be able to kiss their bride." The officiate motioned to the happy newlyweds. "I now pronounce you husbands and wife. You may kiss your bride."

Wes gave Ellie a soft, lingering kiss. He kept his lips touching hers, breathing in her scent. He opened his eyes and found her staring at him, joy radiating from her eyes. With his head pulled back, he brought her hand up to his lips. "I love you, Ellie."

"And I you," Ellie whispered.

Arch tapped Wes on the shoulder. "Move it, bro." Wes gave Arch a good-natured jab to the side as he turned toward their seated friends and family.

He pulled Ellie tight against his body, one hand on her hip and one on her neck. Her head fell back, and she watched his face expectantly. Arch's lips crushed hers, and she had a fleeting thought about the state of her makeup before her mind was overloaded with the feeling of his body touching hers.

Todd let out an exaggerated cough, pulling Ellie and Arch out of their fervor and allowing Gray room to step forward.

Gray, predictably, stole the show. Taking Ellie by the small of her back, he applied pressure so that she arched her back into a dip. While he supported her weight, he bent down and kissed her with soft, eager lips. Instead of invading her mouth with his tongue, he took the moment to whisper more promises to her. "I can't wait to take this gorgeous dress off of you," he said against her lips. "I will unbutton those thousand buttons down your back slowly, until you are aching with anticipation. Just a few more hours, *amante*."

Wes walked around Ellie and pressed himself to her back when Gray stood her upright. "I thought you might need some support after whatever Gray just said to you."

"After those three kisses, I absolutely did." Ellie leaned against Wes, her new husband.

Arch took one hand, and Gray took the other.

The officiate turned to their gathered friends and family. "This new family has decided to take Ellie's name, rather than trying to decide which of their names she should take. May I present to you, Mr. Beaumont-Asche, Mr. Morales-Asche, Mr. Lawson-Asche, and *Mrs.* Asche. Please join me in wishing that they live happily ever after."

ABOUT THE AUTHOR

L.A. Boruff lives in East Tennessee with her husband, three children, and an ever growing number of cats. She loves reading, watching TV, and procrastinating by browsing Facebook. L.A.'s passions include vampires, food, and listening to heavy metal music. She once won a Harry Potter trivia contest based on the books, and lost one based on the movies. She has two bands on her bucket list that she still hasn't seen: AC/DC and Alice Cooper. Feel free to send tickets.